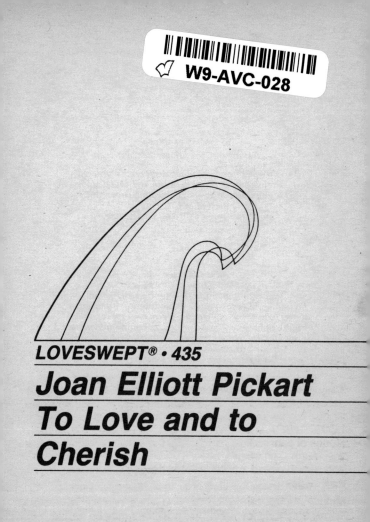

LOVESWEPT® • 435

Joan Elliott Pickart
To Love and to Cherish

BANTAM BOOKS
NEW YORK • TORONTO • LONDON • SYDNEY • AUCKLAND

TO LOVE AND TO CHERISH

A Bantam Book / November 1990

*LOVESWEPT® and the wave device are registered
trademarks of Bantam Books, a division of
Bantam Doubleday Dell Publishing Group, Inc.
Registered in U.S. Patent
and Trademark Office and elsewhere.*

*If you would be interested in receiving protective vinyl
covers for your Loveswept books, please write to this address
for information:*

*Loveswept
Bantam Books
P.O. Box 985
Hicksville, NY 11802*

ISBN 0-553-44066-7

Published simultaneously in the United States and Canada

*Bantam Books are published by Bantam Books, a division
of Bantam Doubleday Dell Publishing Group, Inc. Its trademark, consisting of the words "Bantam Books" and the
portrayal of a rooster, is Registered in U.S. Patent and
Trademark Office and in other countries. Marca Registrada.
Bantam Books, 666 Fifth Avenue, New York, New York 10103.*

PRINTED IN THE UNITED STATES OF AMERICA

OPM   0 9 8 7 6 5 4 3 2 1

In memory of
Jan Milella

Prologue

The fog rolled in off the ocean like great puffs of marshmallow, wrapping the already-warm beach in a comforting blanket. It hushed the sound of the water lapping against the shore, and muffled the night noises from a nearby road.

The beach was so encased in a white cocoon of privacy, the world beyond might not have existed. Only the fog, like clouds dropped from the heavens, was visible in all directions.

The woman walked slowly along the moist sand, wrapped by the mist and her own gloomy thoughts. There was a strange aura to the night, she mused, an otherworldliness. She felt as if she were hiding in the fog, like a child who pulled the covers over her head to keep the ghosts at bay.

Stopping abruptly, she turned to face the water she couldn't see. Her arms wrapped around her waist, she held on tightly, as though to keep herself from shattering into a million jagged pieces.

She drew an unsteady breath, then pressed her lips together to hold back threatening tears.

In the next instant she dropped her hands, curling her fingers into tight fists, and kicked the heavy, damp sand with one tennis-shoe-clad foot. She turned and stomped down the beach for several feet, then retraced her steps a moment later.

Back and forth . . . back and forth. Pacing. Emotions of anger, frustration, self-disgust, and sorrow warred within her, each seeking supremacy. They slammed one into the next, churning, building.

An errant tear slid down one cheek, and she dashed it away with a jerky motion. Still she paced. The tension emanating from her seemed to slice through the thick fog like a sharply honed knife.

Back and forth . . . back and forth.

"Oh, Lord, I'm so stupid," she said, not realizing she'd spoken aloud. "When will I learn? When? Darn it. . . . No, *dammit*. I'm such an idiot. This is April first . . ." Her voice trembled as she fought once more against the tears. "And I'm the greatest fool of all."

"No," a man said. "*I'm* the greatest fool."

She gasped and spun around in the direction of that deep voice. Shock and fear born of the realization that she was no longer alone, that there was a man on that fog-shrouded beach, caused her heart to race painfully fast.

A tall man with wide shoulders and long legs strode toward her, stopping a short distance away. Mist swirled between them, hazing the features of his face. But his voice rang clear and true.

"I'm sorry if I frightened you," he said. "I didn't expect anyone to be out here on a night like this." He laughed—a sharp, humorless sound. "Not only are you here, but you've claimed my title of being the greatest fool."

"There's room, I suppose," she said tentatively, "for two fools."

"I suppose." He took a step toward her.

"No," she said quickly, "stay there, please. I should leave because . . . But if you don't come closer I won't see— Oh, I'm being silly. I really must go."

"No, don't." He held out a hand as if to stop her. "I won't move an inch, I swear it. Please don't go." He paused. "What's your name?"

"I'm— No. No names, all right? We're just two people in the fog. Two people who have agreed to share the title of being the greatest fool."

"You don't sound like a fool."

She sighed wearily. "Oh, but I am."

"I heard what you said. I didn't mean to eavesdrop but . . . You sounded so angry at yourself, yet I heard sorrow in your voice too. I feel the same way. Angry, frustrated, and depressed as hell." He turned to face the murmuring ocean. "This is my fortieth birthday. I think the title of being the greatest fool is rightfully mine, since I was born on April first. I'll share the title with you, but I seriously doubt that you've earned it."

"Oh, I've earned it, all right." She drew in a deep breath of the moist, salty air, hoping it might clear her head. It didn't, and she threw up her hands in frustration. "I have so many emotions hammering at me. I don't know what to do with them all. I want to scream at the top of my lungs. Or rage in fury. Or cry until I don't have one more tear to shed. No, no tears. I *won't* cry. I refuse to dissolve into a weeping puddle."

She shook her head. "Ignore me. I'm blithering, and you obviously have your own problems to deal with. I'll leave the beach to you. Maybe you'll find comfort in this fog." She paused. "It's such a strange night," she added musingly, "as though the mist has swept this place beyond reality."

"We brought reality with us."

"Yes, that's true. I must go." She turned away, but his voice stopped her.

"Look, let me walk you to your car. You shouldn't be out here alone."

"I didn't think about the danger," she said. "I just ended up here. The fog seemed peaceful at first, but then everything came rushing back. There's nowhere to hide, is there?"

"No. Come on, I'll see you safely to your car."

He walked toward her, stopping to stand directly in front of her. Fog still danced between them, and even though they stared at each other for a timeless moment, they discerned only parts of the other's face. His strong jaw, the sweet curve of her cheek; his dark brows, her parted lips.

As one, they turned and started slowly down the beach.

"I'd listen if you want to talk about what's troubling you," the man said finally.

"No. Thank you, but no. Would *you* like to discuss your problems?"

"No, not really. Spilling it out won't change a damn thing. I wish I could help you, though. You seem to be so sad and angry at yourself. I don't know. I just hate the idea you might leave here, then cry when you're alone. Why don't you talk to me?"

She shook her head. "Don't. Don't be nice

to me. I'm an emotional mess, a total wreck, and if you leave me be, my anger will see me through this." Her voice trembled. "But if you're kind and comforting . . . Please, just don't say another word."

"Hey." He slipped one arm around her shoulders. "The last thing I want to do is upset you further." They stopped walking and he eased her close to his side. "I just want you to know that I'm here for you. You're not alone."

She let out a long sigh, straining for control, then burst into tears. Covering her face with her hands, she gave way to the sobs that shuddered through her.

"Oh, Lord," he muttered, wrapping his arms around her and nestling her to him. "Now I've done it."

Not even considering the oddness of her accepting comfort from a complete stranger, she rested against him and allowed her sorrow and hurt to overflow. In some dim corner of her mind she realized that her ease with this man was thoroughly uncharacteristic of her, but she wouldn't worry about that now. She simply cried. She cried until she was exhausted, until the tears, like a cleansing rain, washed away—at least temporarily—the fury of emotions within her.

As her sobs finally quieted, the man continued to hold her, trying to give her as much warmth and comfort as he could. His own problems were forgotten as he centered his concern on the woman he held.

With a last gasp she stopped crying, and awkwardly brushed the tears from her face. She drew in a deep, calming breath, and smelled not just the salt of the ocean, but a man's tantalizing cologne. Her hand dropped away from her face, and of its own volition came to rest on his chest. Beneath it, she could feel his heart beating, strong, steady . . . and quickening ever so slightly. Unconsciously, she stirred against him, seeking even more of his warmth, one arm sliding around his waist. He inhaled sharply, then his own arms tightened around her.

Her heart pounded hard, her breath caught in her throat, and she looked up at him.

He lowered his head, and their lips met.

Desire exploded within them with the force of a rocket, and passion consumed them instantly. As his tongue met hers, stroking, dueling, dancing, he fit her to the cradle of his lips, crushing her small breasts against his chest.

They were going up in flames, burning . . . burning . . . burning . . .

She clung to him as her trembling legs threatened to give way beneath her, and his muscles tautened in her grasp. His hands roamed over her back, down to her buttocks, then upward again to tangle in the silken strands of her hair.

He drank of her like a thirsty man, like a bee finding the sweet nectar of a flower known to no other. She fit against him like the missing piece to a puzzle, like the woman he'd been unknowingly searching for, and had at last found.

Never before had either known such need, such raging passion. Yet intertwined with the sensual ecstasy was a sense of peace, of completeness, of having traveled far and come home. Warmth, as soothing as the summer sun after a cold rain, chased away the chilling loneliness that had darkened their lives. Their spirits soared, and they were filled with joy.

The magical night had been created just for them. This was their moment out of time. They had no past, no future. There was only now.

"Oh, God," the man said hoarsely, "I want you. I want you so damn much."

"I want you too," she whispered.

"Are you sure? Please, this is important. I have to know that you—"

"Shh. This is our night. Yes, I'm sure this is what I want, *you* are what I want. There's no world beyond this mist. Everything has disappeared but the two of us."

"No." He cupped her face in his hands,

staring into her eyes, frustrated that the night and the fog hid so much of her from him. "Listen to me—"

"Make love with me," she said, and pressed her lips to his.

With a groan he lifted her into his arms and carried her toward a huge rock. The fog seemed to part as he moved, showing him the way to a thick carpet of grass behind the stone.

He laid her gently on the ground as the mist closed around them again, then stretched out next to her. His mouth melted over hers, as he slid one hand beneath her sweater. Her skin was soft, like the whisper of dew on a meadow at dawn. His fingers inched upward to cup a breast covered in wispy lace. His tongue delved deeper into her mouth, and a purr of pleasure escaped from her throat.

Their clothes seemed to float away as they eagerly kissed and caressed each other. The undeniable sense of rightness as they pressed their naked bodies together washed away any awkwardness, any hesitation. As he kissed her breast, laving the nipple with his tongue to bring it to a taut point, she wondered fleetingly at how such pure ecstasy could arise so unexpectedly, could explode so swiftly. Then her thoughts were shattered as he drew her soft flesh into his mouth, sucking, savoring.

"Oh," she whispered, gasping. "Oh, yes."

He shifted to her other breast as one of his hands slid down her body, over her flat belly to find her moist heat. As he tortured her sweetly, his manhood surged against her thigh, aching, wanting.

"Please, oh, please," she cried out.

"Yes," he murmured.

He moved over her, then entered her slowly, a moan of pleasure rumbling in his chest. She wrapped her legs around his thighs and urged him on as she sank her hands into his thick hair.

Deeper, deeper within her he went. He claimed her mouth in a hard, searing kiss, then began to love her with a rhythm she matched, beat for pounding beat. Harder, faster, he surged within her, his body glistening as the coiling heat gathered force inside him. She lifted her hips and he drove deeper still. Waves of tightening tension swept through them, centering in the place where there was no discerning him from her.

And then with a thundering crash they were flung into the abyss, clinging to each other.

He threw back his head, a moan of pure satisfaction echoing from him as his life's force surged into her. Then he collapsed against her, spent, sated. With his last ounce of energy he rolled onto his back, taking her with him, their bodies still joined.

Neither spoke.

The mist swirled around them with its comforting warmth as their bodies cooled and their heartbeats quieted.

Sighing, she nestled her face in the crook of his neck. She was awed by the contentment and fulfillment she felt, and again wondered at the magic of the night.

"Oh, my," she said at last.

He chuckled softly, his body rocking beneath hers.

"Am I too heavy?"

"You're as light as a butterfly. "You're . . . you're the stamp and I'm the envelope."

She smiled. "A stamp and an envelope? Is that romantic?"

"Sure, because we've decided it is. It has a secret romantic meaning just for the two of us. A stamp and an envelope, that's who we are."

"Perfect."

They were silent again for a few minutes, lost in their own thoughts.

"Please tell me why you came here tonight," he said finally. "What happened to cause you such pain?"

Her hold on him tightened, as though knowing he was there gave her the courage to speak.

"I threw caution to the wind and loved," she said quietly, "and I chose the wrong man. We worked at the same hotel, you see, and he was sent to Europe to open a new one a few weeks after we got engaged. He was gone for six months, and today he came back to tell me he'd fallen in love with a woman he met over there."

"Then he's the fool."

"I shouldn't have dared to love," she went on as though he hadn't spoken. "All my life I've known the dangers of caring, of loving. My own mother had no use for me. Her men, that's what was important to her. Man after man after man. But I was so sure that Carl was right for me, that this time . . ." Her voice trailed off.

"Did you love him very much?" the man asked.

"Yes, of course." She shook her head, her hair brushing against his shoulder. "No, this is a night for the truth, and after—after what we've shared, I can't lie to you.

"In the six months that Carl was gone, I began to forget what he looked like, what his voice, his laughter, sounded like. I tried to hold on to my feelings for him, but they kept slipping away. I wanted to love him, be a part of his life and end the years of loneliness, but . . . oh, God, it's so clear to me now. I was lying to myself about Carl. I wasn't meant to love him, or anyone. I know that now."

"No, you're wrong about that," the man said, turning his head so he could look at her. "You didn't choose well, that's all. I'm the greater fool because I've never loved at all. Years of loneliness? I know all about those. This is my fortieth birthday, and in spite of my wealth I have nothing that matters, no one to share my life with. I want to love, and you should too. Loneliness is hell. I guess my biggest fear is that it's too late for me, that I've missed my chance of finding her, that special woman."

She rose up slightly to gaze into his night-darkened eyes. "Oh, no, you mustn't think that. It's not too late for you. You want to love, and your heart will listen. You know now that you have to slow down, pay atten-tion to today so you won't run the risk of her passing you by." Her gaze dropped. "And I must be sure to do just the opposite, to never again lower my guard. How different we are, you and I."

"Are we?" he said. "We're both very lonely people."

"But I'll accept my loneliness, and you'll do something about changing yours. I wish you well. I hope . . . no, I know you'll find her."

"You believe in love for everyone but your-self?"

"Yes, I guess that's how I feel." She paused. "How very strange this night is. I don't talk to anyone about my inner thoughts. I'm not behaving like myself at all, but I'm not sorry we made love."

He lifted a hand and drew his thumb lightly over her cheek. "Exquisitely soft," he said. "Like the petal of a flower." He smiled. "I should snap my fingers and make a bottle of champagne appear out of nowhere."

"To celebrate your birthday?"

"To celebrate us, this night, what took place here in the fog."

"You *are* a romantic."

"Well, no one has ever said that before, but I guess maybe I am, given the right circumstances. With the proper lady, of course."

"The champagne would be lovely, but I can't drink anything like that without getting a terrible case of hiccups. I have ginger ale with a cherry in it at parties so everyone thinks I'm actually having hard liquor. It's just easier than explaining my childish hiccups. There. Now you know a deep, dark secret about me."

"Indeed I do. And fair is fair. What deep, dark secret of mine . . . Ah, this is a good one. I'm so petrified of going to the dentist that they have to give me laughing gas. There, I've confessed. Is that an even trade for your hiccups?"

She laughed softly, rejoicing in the delicious wave of contentment and happiness that swept through her. "I'd say that's a very even trade."

They talked on in low, lazy voices, comparing their choices of favorite movies, books, hobbies. They became lost in the sharing of their lives, until a sudden chilling breeze whipped over them. She shivered.

"Hey, you're cold," he said.

Before she could reply, he grasped her waist and gently lifted her off him, setting her next to him on the grass.

"I'm not really cold," she said as he handed her her sweater. Another shiver betrayed her.

"Yes, you are, and I'm hungry." He began to pull on his clothes, and she did the same. "We'll go get something to eat, all right? I want to see you, really see you." They got to their feet, and he placed his hands gently on her shoulders. "Please, tell me your name. It's due and overdue, don't you think?"

She stiffened and blinked, as though coming out of a trance. Quickly stepping back, she forced him to drop his hands.

"No," she said, her voice trembling. "No, I won't tell you my name, and I don't want to know yours. Oh, please, don't ruin this magical night. It was so special, so wonderful, and I just want to remember it exactly as it was. You're the man of the mist. I'm the woman of the mist. There's nothing more to say."

"Nothing more to say?" he repeated incredulously, his brows drawing together in a frown. "We have a million things to say to each other. Dammit, this is just the beginning for us."

She shook her head wildly. "No. No."

"You said yourself that this night was special." he said, his voice rising. "And now what? You just walk out of my life as though none of this actually happened?"

"It was special, yes, but not real. Can't you see that? Don't you understand? We're two lonely people who met in the mist and shared something incredibly beautiful. But it's over now. Good-bye." A sob caught in her throat. "Happy birthday."

She turned and ran, disappearing instantly in the thick fog.

"No!" he yelled. "Wait. Please!"

He started after her, then stopped. He had no idea which direction she'd gone, and it would be impossible to find her in the fog.

"But I *will* find you," he said quietly, staring into the white night. "I swear to heaven that I'll find you."

One

Paul-Anthony Payton sat at his large mahogany desk, studying a file. Hearing a light drum-roll knock on his open office door, he glanced up. A tall, broad-shouldered man leaned against the frame of the door. Paul-Anthony sprang to his feet.

Any stranger would have known the men were related. Their builds and handsome faces were similar, and their blue eyes were nearly identical. The most striking difference between the two was their thick hair; Paul-Anthony's was black with threads of gray at the temples, the other man's a rich, burnished shade of dark auburn.

"Speak, John-Trevor," Paul-Anthony said gruffly, "and I hope to hell you're not here to report . . . again . . . that you haven't found her. Dammit, man, it's been six weeks."

John-Trevor grinned and raised his hands in a gesture of peace as he pushed away from the door. He crossed the room and settled onto one of the chairs opposite Paul-Anthony's desk.

"You're too stressed out," John-Trevor said, still smiling. "Hey, big brother, you're dealing with the head of the finest security firm on the West Coast. My company does everything from installing burglar alarms to providing bodyguards for the rich and famous to—"

"Could I pass on the commercial for Payton Security?" Paul-Anthony interrupted, sitting back down. He closed his eyes and squeezed the bridge of his nose, then looked at his brother again. "So, go ahead. Fill me in on all the leads that didn't pan out this time."

"This wasn't an easy assignment," John-Trevor said. "You didn't give me much to go on."

"The hell I didn't. How many hotel chains could have opened a new branch in Europe in the past year?"

"Four. I told you that. Our brilliant baby brother, James-Steven, was able to get that information since he owns the Castle hotels in this country. Everything else has been old-fashioned legwork, Paul-Anthony. All I've had is your . . . a-hem, foggy description of her—

she's slender, about five-six, has wavy shoulder-length hair, although you don't know what color—and the fact that she works in a hotel in this area. Somewhere. I didn't know how far she had driven that night to get to the beach. The four hotels that opened European branches are close enough to make them all viable candidates. Plus, we didn't know what she does at the hotel."

"Okay, okay," Paul-Anthony said, "but six weeks? Lord, John-Trevor, she's out there somewhere."

"Yep," he said, appearing very pleased with himself, "and I found her."

Paul-Anthony was on his feet again, his hands planted flat on the desk as he leaned toward John-Trevor.

"You found her? Don't play games with me, John-Trevor, I'm not in the mood."

"You've been in a lousy mood for six weeks." He took a small notebook from his shirt pocket. "Sit."

Paul-Anthony sat.

"Your lady," John Trevor said, flipping the notebook open, "is the conference and meeting director for the Swan Hotel off Wilshire here in L.A."

Paul-Anthony's heartbeat quickened. "My God, you've actually done it. You've found her."

"Of course. I usually assign missing person

cases to one of my detectives, but I handled this myself with awesome expertise."

"What is her name?"

"Alida Hunter."

"Alida. Ah-lie-da." Paul-Anthony repeated the lovely name slowly. It seemed to echo through his mind, his heart, his very soul. "Alida. Yes."

"She's twenty-nine, has worked at the Swan for five years, and was promoted to director a year ago, having previously been assistant director of conferences and meetings. She lives in a high-rise apartment with a cat named Scooter. And"—John-Trevor smiled—"she is one very beautiful woman."

"I know," Paul-Anthony said quietly. "I never saw her face clearly, but I know."

"She was engaged to Carl Ambrey, but you know the story on that. She's never been arrested, got one speeding ticket three years ago, and had a pizza delivered to her apartment for dinner last night. She drove to work this morning in her late-model red compact car, and was in her office at eight o'clock sharp." He snapped the notebook shut. "I'll give you her address. The ball, Paul-Anthony, is now in your court."

"Thank you, John-Trevor. I mean that sincerely. I've been going out of my mind these past six weeks, but now . . . well, thanks."

John-Trevor frowned and leaned forward, resting his elbows on his knees.

"Paul-Anthony, you and I were very happy for James-Steven when he married Maggie. They worked through the problems in their relationship and they're great together. Seeing James-Steven with Maggie reaffirmed in my mind that I'm not now, nor will I ever be, the type of guy to settle down, get married, make a lifelong commitment."

Paul-Anthony nodded. "What you're saying doesn't surprise me, but I get the feeling you're trying to make a point."

"I am. I think . . . maybe . . . that you had the opposite reaction to James-Steven and Maggie getting married, that you began to realize that you *did* want what they have. Then you did all that soul-searching on your birthday, depressed the hell out of yourself, and there she was in the fog, seemingly waiting for you."

"And?"

"And I'm concerned that you've blown it all out of proportion over the past six weeks. Get angry if you want, Paul-Anthony, but I had to say what was on my mind."

Paul-Anthony gazed at his brother for a long moment before speaking.

"I understand what you're saying," he said at last, "and I appreciate the fact that you're disturbed about the situation. It's not, shall we say, ordinary. But, John-Trevor, my life totally changed on that beach. As unbelievable as it sounds, even to myself sometimes, I fell in love with Alida Hunter that night. She's mine."

John-Trevor shook his head and got to his feet. "Well, good luck. Keep me posted."

"I will, and thanks again."

"I just hope you don't come to regret that I found her. From what I've heard, broken hearts are not a thrill a minute."

"Everything is going to be fine," Paul-Anthony said. "I'll talk to you later."

"Yeah, okay." John-Trevor left the office.

"Everything is going to be fine," Paul-Anthony repeated to the empty room. "Alida Hunter is mine, my lady of the mist. Forever."

"Hello, hello," Alida Hunter's secretary said, opening Alida's office door.

"Good-bye, good-bye," Alida said, smiling at the attractive, dark-haired woman. "Have a nice evening, Lisa."

"As your secretary," Lisa said, "it's part of my duty to tell you that our workday is over and it's time to go home. Your handy-dandy assistant, Jerry, just exited stage left, and I'm right behind him."

Alida laughed. "I'm going too, I promise. There are just a couple of things I want to double-check, then I'm on my way."

"Well, all right. I'll trust you not to burn the midnight oil."

"You're an old fuss-budget, considering

you're only twenty-five years old, Lisa Donovan. Now, shoo. The sooner you quit nagging at me, the sooner I'll be out of here."

"I'm gone. I'll leave this door open and the outer one unlocked, as usual."

"And I'll lock up behind me, mother," Alida said. "Good night."

" 'Night," Lisa said, and left.

A heavy silence fell over her office, and Alida leaned back in her chair with a sigh. Fatigue washed over her as she closed her eyes.

She was almost unbearably tired, she thought. She'd give herself five minutes of doing nothing, and hope that she didn't fall asleep. It would be so easy to drift off into a lovely fog of oblivion and—

Alida's eyes popped open and she straightened in her chair.

Darn it, she fumed. Fog. And the man she'd met in the mist. He was filling her mind once more, the events of that night crystal-clear in every detail. She could envision him standing before her again, his face and form shadowed by fog; could hear his voice; could relive the ecstasy of becoming one with him, an ecstasy that surpassed everything she'd ever known.

He was haunting her day and night, and along with her memories of that night was an ever-increasing humiliation at her behavior.

Lord, she thought, shaking her head, it

was still so unbelievable. Miss Prim-and-Proper Alida Hunter had made love with a total stranger. She'd divulged her innermost feelings, told him of her private pain, then . . .

How long, she wondered, was it going to take for the memories to fade, then finally disappear? How long before the hold this stranger had on her loosened and fell away? It had been six weeks, yet it might as well have been six hours. When would she be free of him and the memories?

Alida sighed again, then forced herself to concentrate on the papers on her desk. Soon she was deeply engrossed in cross-checking lists, assuring herself that preparations for next week's day-long high school teacher's seminar were all under control.

Suddenly, out of nowhere, a plain white envelope appeared on top of the papers. An instant later, a single stamp floated down on top of it.

"Hello, Alida."

She gasped and snapped her head up. Her heart raced, and she could feel the color drain from her face.

Dear Lord, no! she thought in horror. He was there, standing in front of her desk, the man of the mist. She'd heard his voice echoing endlessly in her mind during the past weeks.

"No," she whispered, staring at him with wide eyes.

"Yes. It wasn't easy finding you, but I finally managed it."

"Why?" she asked. "What do you want with me?"

"Don't you know?"

"No. What happened was—was wrong. I'm terribly ashamed of my behavior."

Dear heaven, she thought, he was even more magnificent than she'd imagined. His thick hair was as dark as a raven's wing, with threads of silver sprinkled at the temples. His features were rugged and strong, bronzed by the sun; not at all pretty-boy perfect, but intriguingly attractive. His eyes were as blue as a summer sky, and framed in long, dark lashes. And his mouth . . . she trembled, remembering the feel of it on hers.

He was so handsome and distinguished, wearing a tailored steel-gray suit. Strength and power emanated from him, yet she knew he could be gentle . . .

"That night wasn't real," she said. "It was strange, like something from another world. Go away. Leave me alone."

"No," he said.

"Yes!" She waved a hand over the stamp and envelope. "And take those with you. I don't want any reminders of what I did."

Strawberry-blond, Paul-Anthony thought. The silken hair he'd tangled his fingers in was strawberry-blond. She had the biggest brown eyes he'd ever seen, and her lips were perfect. Made for kissing, made for sharing *his* kisses. He now knew the true meaning of a peaches-and-cream complexion, because he was staring at one. She was such a beautiful woman. And she was his.

He planted his hands flat on the desk and leaned toward her. Despite herself, Alida moved back, feeling trapped by his massive form, by his very presence.

"Alida," he said, his voice low, "I have no intention of walking out of here and disappearing from your life. I've spent six weeks trying to find you because what happened between us on that foggy beach was fantastic, wonderful, and very, very important."

"It was disgraceful." She lifted her chin. "I've dismissed it from my mind, haven't given it a moment's thought. If you were a gentleman, you'd do the same."

Paul-Anthony chuckled and straightened, crossing his arms over his chest.

She was really something, he mused. She was everything and more that he remembered her to be. And she was his. Yet it was becoming very apparent, very quickly, that convincing Alida Hunter of the fact was not going to be easy.

"Now," she said, "if you'll excuse me. Mr.—Mr. Whoever You Are, I'd like to finish my work. Good-bye."

"My name is Paul-Anthony Payton, and I own Payton Investment Corporation. I just had my fortieth birthday but, of course, you know that. I've never been married, as I said that night on the beach, but I've decided it's definitely time that I was. Do you like children? I hope so, because I'd like to have a couple. I have two brother's John-Trevor and James-Steven. We all have hyphenated names because our mother was French and liked hyphenated names. My parents are no longer living. I own a large house, two cars, and a Jeep, I don't smoke, and I drink only on a social basis. Oh, and I have all my own teeth. We covered favorite movies, books, and the like the night we met. Is there anything else you'd like to know about me?"

"Yes," she said sweetly. "Did you get a day pass from the funny farm, or did you escape?"

He blinked in surprise at her unexpected response, then threw his head back and roared with laughter, the deep, rich resonance seeming to fill the room to overflowing.

As his laughter and smile faded, he walked slowly around her desk to tower above her. His expression serious, he gripped the arms of her chair and leaned down until his face was only inches from hers.

"Alida," he said, his voice and gaze mesmerizing, "you told me that night on the beach that I should slow down, pay attention, so that the special woman who was meant to be mine wouldn't pass me by unnoticed. That's exactly what I'm doing. I've found her, that special lady, and her name is Alida Hunter. I have no intention of losing you. I've been lonely too long. You're mine, or you will be as soon as you quit fighting me. Think about that night, Alida. Remember how it was between us, what we shared. We joined our minds, hearts, and souls with our deepest secrets. We joined our bodies with the most exquisite lovemaking I've ever experienced. You do remember, Alida, don't you?"

Heat throbbed deep within Alida as she was held immobile by Paul-Anthony's blue gaze. As vivid pictures of their encounter in the fog flashed before her eyes, her heart raced and a flush stained her cheeks.

She had only to lean forward a few inches, she realized, and her lips would meet his. She had only to lift her hands to touch him once again, to feel the power in his tightly muscled body. His aroma, his enticing, familiar male aroma, was filling her senses, evoking sensuous memories.

He was so close . . . so close.

Stop it! she told herself. He had to go. He had to leave and allow her to forget her uncharacteristic, unacceptable behavior of that eerie, otherworldly night. She would not grant Paul-Anthony Payton entrance into her real life. He was dangerous, his invisible hold on her frightening. She would *not* be swept away by his magnetism. She would *not* lose her heart to Paul-Anthony, or to any other man. Not ever again.

"Tell me, Alida," he said, "that you remember every detail of our hours together on that beach."

"No," she said, but her voice was trembling slightly. "I told you that I've dismissed it from my mind as though it never happened."

"Then I guess I'll just have to refresh your memory."

"No, I don't want— Oh!" She gasped as he grasped her upper arms and lifted her to her feet. "No, stop it. I—"

Her protest was halted by his mouth melting over hers, his tongue parting her lips. He dropped his hands to wrap his arms around her, bringing her tightly against him.

Alida flattened her hands on his chest and pushed, but she was no match for Paul-Anthony's strength. The kiss deepened, and before she knew she had done it, her hands clasped his neck and she returned the searing kiss with six weeks' worth of frustrated desire.

Oh, yes, she thought, he was there. After six long, empty, lonely weeks, he had come. This was the kiss, the taste, the very essence of him that she remembered, and, oh, how she'd missed him. She burned with the re-kindled need for him, and felt truly alive for the first time since that night. Yes, he was there.

Paul-Anthony raised his head, and his breathing was rough, his eyes smoky gray with desire.

"Alida," he said, hoarsely, "I've waited an eternity to kiss you and hold you again. But those weeks are behind us now, and we're together as we should be. Alida, I have to tell you. I fell in love with you that night in the fog. I love you, Alida Hunter."

The hazy, dreamlike spell that had floated over Alida dissipated so quickly, she was struck by a brief wave of dizziness.

"What?" she whispered.

"I could hardly believe it myself at first because it happened so quickly. But it's true, and to say I'm happy about it doesn't begin to express how I feel. I do love you, Alida."

She slid her hands down to his chest again and pushed, catching him off-guard enough that he had to take a steadying step back-ward. She slipped past him and strode to the door.

"I would like you to leave, Mr. Payton," she said stiffly.

"Alida, listen to me. I know you've been badly hurt in the past, that you're determined never to love again. But what you and I have together is so rare and beautiful. You didn't choose the wrong man this time, because I love you with all that I am. The future, a glorious future, is ours for the taking, to share."

"Go," she said, pointing to the doorway. "And don't come back. I don't want you in my life. Why can't you understand that?"

He crossed the room to stand in front of her. "How do you explain your response to the kiss that just took place?"

"I don't have to explain anything to you. The only thing you need to comprehend is that I never want to see you again. I repeat, go away."

"I'll leave . . . for now. But I *will* be back, Alida."

"No."

"Yes." He trailed his thumb across her kiss-swollen lips, then left the office.

A shiver coursed through Alida, and she wrapped her arms around herself. Sudden tears blurred her vision as she stumbled to one of the chairs in front of her desk. Sinking down into it, she pressed her fingertips to throbbing temples and closed her eyes.

Paul-Anthony's passionately spoken words echoed in her mind and fluttered around her heart.

I fell in love with you that night.

She opened her eyes and leaned back in

the chair, feeling physically and emotionally drained.

I love you, Alida Hunter.

No, she thought, he didn't. He had been swept away by the magical aura of that night on the beach. He did believe, at that point in time, that he was in love with her. He'd proven it by his tenacity, his determination to find her.

But it was temporary, she reasoned. His love would dim, then fade away, along with the memories of that night in the mist. Then, just as Carl had done, Paul-Anthony would move on, find someone else.

But this time, Alida vowed, she was not going to suffer a shattered heart. Not this time. Not ever again.

She would not fall prey to Paul Anthony's declarations of love, nor to his arousing kisses that chased all rational thought from her mind. She would construct a high and sturdy wall around herself, granting him no entry. Soon, he would tire of his useless attempts to gain access to her, and go away and leave her alone.

Alone and lonely.

Alida sighed. She was painting such a bleak picture of her future. Well, it needn't be that way. Love might not be in the cards for her—a lesson she'd learned during her childhood, and again with Carl Ambrey—but she had a challenging career that kept her busy and gave her a tremendous sense of accomplishment. She had a good income, a lovely apartment, and funny little Scooter, her cat, who was so glad to see her at day's end.

She had women friends to go shopping or out to lunch with, and although she hadn't felt like dating since Carl ended their engagement, several attractive men had shown an interest in her.

Yes, she was doing fine. She had all she needed for a full, well-rounded life.

I love you, Alida Hunter.

"No," she said aloud. "I don't want to hear it. As of this moment, Paul-Anthony Payton, you're totally and absolutely out of my thoughts and out of my life."

"So, Dr. Allen," Alida said to her family practitioner the next morning, after the doctor had examined her, "I figure I may be getting awfully tired lately simply because I've been working very hard." And not sleeping well, she added silently, because of the damnable haunting dreams of Paul-Anthony Payton. "But since I was anemic for a spell last year, I thought I'd better play it safe and come to see you. What's the verdict? Am I back to popping iron pills?"

Dr. Tracy Allen rested her elbows on the

arms of her chair and made a steeple of her fingers. She studied Alida for a long, silent moment, then dropped her hands to the top of her desk.

"No," she said, "your blood count is fine."

"Well, that's good news. I guess I'll chalk up my fatigue to the fact that I'll be thirty on my next birthday. So goes the energy of youth."

"Alida," Dr. Allen said quietly, "you're pregnant."

Alida stared at the doctor as though she'd never seen her before in her life.

"You didn't suspect anything?" Dr. Allen asked.

"No," Alida said weakly. "No. My cycle has always been erratic and . . . dear heaven."

A baby, she thought, incredulously. She was going to have Paul-Anthony Payton's baby! Oh, Lord, no.

"I can't believe this. I . . ." She shook her head.

"At this early stage in pregnancy," Dr. Allen said, "we can only estimate how far along you are, but I would say six to eight weeks."

"Yes. Six weeks . . . It's been that long . . . A baby?"

Dr. Allen smiled. "Most definitely." She paused and her smile faded. "Alida, this has obviously come as a complete shock to you, and I think you need some time to let it sink in. I'd like to suggest that you make an appointment to see me next week and we'll discuss it further. Of course, it may just be a simple matter of telling the father and—"

"No," Alida interrupted. "He mustn't know. Not ever."

"It *is* his child too," Dr. Allen said gently.

Alida pressed one hand to her flushed forehead. "No, it isn't. I mean, it is but . . . no. Oh, it's all so complicated. You're right. I need some time to think. I'll—I'll see you next week." She rushed to the door. "Good-bye."

"Good-bye," Dr. Allen said, frowning.

Alida stopped at a small café several blocks from the hotel and ordered a cup of tea. She was not prepared to go to work yet, to slip into her role of the highly efficient executive.

A baby, she thought, still dazed. She was going to have a baby that had been conceived with Paul-Anthony on that magical night. Paul-Anthony Payton, who had appeared in her office the previous evening, was the father of this tiny miracle nestled deep within her. Oh, dear Lord, what was she going to do?

"Your tea," the waitress said, bringing Alida from her reverie. "Will there be anything else?"

Answers to a million questions, Alida thought. And a hug. A warm, everything-is-going-to-be-all-right hug. "No, thank you."

"Have a nice day," the woman said, placing the check on the table.

A nice day? Alida repeated silently. What about the rest of her life? She was going to have a baby, for heaven's sake, and she was terrified.

But then again . . . The baby would be hers to love and cherish and tend to. Didn't children return unconditionally the love they received? For the first time in her life she would give and receive love in its purest form.

They would be wonderful together, she thought dreamily, her and her child. There would be a special bond between them, hours of sharing, caring, and endless hugs. They would be a family, the two of them. And Scooter, of course.

And Paul-Anthony Payton? her mind taunted. "It is his child too," Dr. Allen had said. Clinically speaking, yes, Alida argued. But this child had been created in a mystical moment, an interlude in time that had no link with reality. The baby was real and would remain, to Alida, separate and apart from the foggy night and the man of the mist.

She slid out of the booth and picked up the check. As she left the café, she was smiling.

When Alida entered her office, Lisa sighed with relief.

"Thank goodness you're here," the secretary said. "His highness has been storming the gates looking for you. I told him you had an early appointment and would be a little late, but try telling Max Brewer to have patience. I wish he'd transfer to a Swan hotel in Siberia and be the manager there."

Alida smiled. "There isn't a Swan in Siberia."

"They should build one just for Brewer to manage! Anyway, you'd better hustle to his office before he has a total fit. He's had Jerry held captive in there for fifteen minutes. Oh, and good morning."

"Good morning to you too," Alida said. "I wasn't sure for a while that it was, but during a calming cup of tea I realized that it's a very good morning indeed."

"It's nice to see you so chipper, Alida. I mean, after the way that louse, Carl Ambrey—No, don't get me started. I'm erasing Ambrey from my memory bank."

"Sounds fine to me. I'm off to his lordship's domain."

Max Brewer was in his late fifties, with thinning hair and a florid complexion that gave evidence of many three-martini lunches and dinners over the years. He was twenty pounds overweight, smoked continually, and, Alida was convinced, had long since forgotten how to smile, if he'd ever known how.

Jerry Nash, Alida's handsome thirty-two-year-old assistant, smiled at her as she entered Max's office, and rolled his eyes when Max wasn't looking. She returned the smile, then sobered as she sat in the chair next to him.

"Hello, Max," she said pleasantly. "I understand you wanted to see me."

"It's about time you got here," Max said gruffly. "This is important, a real feather in the Swan cap, and a client like this one should never be kept waiting. He left to wander around the lobby until you showed up."

"I had no appointments scheduled here this morning," Alida said, determined not to sound defensive.

"A man like this doesn't need an appointment," Max said. "I tried to get him to start going over details with Jerry, but no dice."

Alida glanced at Jerry, who just shrugged.

"He wants a conference held here in two months," Max went on, "of his key people and some of their wives from his branch offices across the country. I'd think he'd assign some assistant to work with us, but he's personally handling the initial setup. The conference has got to come together perfectly, because other firms of this caliber will be aware of it. It could create a tremendous domino effect, and put us way out in front of the competition. There's no room for error on this, Alida. None. Am I making myself clear?"

"Of course," she said. "We handle every meeting and conference here with meticulous care."

"I want better than that," Max said, pounding a fist once on his desk. "Perfection, Alida. I won't settle for less on this one."

"My goodness," she said, "who *is* this client?"

"Me," a deep voice said from behind her.

She spun around in her chair and her eyes widened.

"Hello," Paul-Anthony said, smiling as he walked into the room. "You must be Alida Hunter. I'm Paul-Anthony Payton, owner of Payton Investment Corporation. It's my conference we're setting up here. You and I, Miss Hunter, are going to be working very closely together for the next couple of months. We're going to be like, shall we say, a stamp and an envelope."

Two

When Alida entered her apartment that evening, she was so weary she was close to tears. As she set her purse on the end table, a blur of black and white fur streaked across the room.

"Hi, Scooter," she said. She picked up the cat and hugged it, receiving a lick on the nose with a sandpapery tongue in return. "Thank you," she said, laughing. "I needed that. Do you want some supper?"

She fed the hungry pet in the kitchen, then went into the bedroom to change into jeans and a yellow terry-cloth top. She started to leave the room, but hesitated and sank onto the edge of the bed instead.

That day, she decided, had been a year

long. Throughout the morning and afternoon, the realization that she was going to have a baby would hit her when she least expected it. She'd shake her head in disbelief, then settle down again with the knowledge that this baby, *her* baby, would be a welcomed and wonderful addition to her life.

She splayed both hands on her stomach as though to feel the tiny entity within her.

"Hello, my baby," she whispered, a soft smile touching her lips.

But her smile faded as the image of Paul-Anthony nudged into her mental vision.

Oh, how clever he had been, she thought, narrowing her eyes. When he'd appeared in Max Brewer's office, he'd pretended he was meeting her for the first time. He'd even shaken her hand, for crying out loud. Still he'd managed, the bum, to get in his zinger about them being as close as a stamp and an envelope, and she'd felt the heat of embarrassment on her cheeks.

He'd been adamant about planning his annual conference personally with Miss Alida Hunter, since she was, after all, the director in charge of such events. Max had nearly fallen over his fat self assuring him that Alida would be at his beck and call. And there she'd sat with a plastic smile on her face agreeing to the whole fiasco. She was to meet Paul-Anthony in her office at nine o'clock the following morning. Darn, darn, darn.

Paul-Anthony Payton, she mused. She really did like his name. It had a powerful sound to it, a ring of authority. His French mother had given hyphenated names to his two brothers, also, and she thought it was romantic and enchanting.

Did his brothers look like him? she wondered absently. Were they as tall and well-built, as handsome? Would the baby she carried take after Paul-Anthony, be a carbon copy of its magnificent father?

Stop it, she told herself. She had to hold firm to her vow that this was *her* baby, and *hers* alone. Paul-Anthony had been a stranger that night, and she would leave him and her memories of their lovemaking encased in the fog, where they belonged. The executive she was meeting the next morning was simply a client of the Swan hotel. She would manage to work with Paul-Anthony on a purely professional level. Somehow.

Alida got to her feet. "Time to eat." She patted her stomach. "And for you, a glass of milk."

The next morning, shortly after Alida had arrived at the hotel, Jerry Nash walked into her office.

"Good morning," she said, smiling at her assistant. "How are you today?"

"I'm fine, but you look rather pale," he said as he sat in a chair opposite her desk.

She *felt* pale, Alida thought dryly. She'd suffered through her first bout of morning sickness that morning, and it had not been a wonderful experience. "I'm all right, just a little tired. It's been hectic around here, with no relief in sight."

"And the big man has an appointment at nine o'clock sharp," Jerry said. "I thought Max was going to come unglued when he realized Paul-Anthony Payton wanted to hold his annual conference here. What I can't figure out is why someone like Payton would be handling this personally, instead of delegating it.

Alida began shuffling papers on her desk, keeping her eyes averted from Jerry's. "I have no idea."

"I guess if you're Paul-Anthony Payton," Jerry went on, "You can do anything you damn well please."

Not quite, Alida thought. Paul-Anthony Payton was *not* going to become part of her life.

"Anyway," Jerry said, "I stopped by to tell you that the reservations for the writers' conference are starting to come in. It's going to be a biggie, just like their coordinator said. They're still planning on roughly two thousand people—authors, editors, agents, booksellers. Max was flying high on having this conference here, until Payton showed up."

"I'm sure Max is still aware of how important the writers' conference is, Jerry. Do we have the proposed meal menus ready for the coordinator to take to her committee?"

Jerry stood up. "That's my next stop. I'm on my way to see if the menus are ready. Good luck with Payton. You know, I could have handled his conference with my eyes closed. I mean, hell, how big can it be? But, oh, no, Mr. Megabucks will work only with you, the director."

"So we go with the flow," Alida said breezily.

Jerry frowned. "Yeah, right. I'll check in with you later."

Oh, good grief, Alida thought, sighing as Jerry left her office. She was going to be an accomplished actress before this was over. Jerry's ego was bruised because Paul-Anthony had not even considered working with him. So she had to put on a golly-gee-whiz attitude, saying she had no idea why Paul-Anthony Payton was so adamant on his stand. Oh, why didn't Paul-Anthony just go away and leave her alone?

I love you, Alida Hunter.

"No," she aloud. "I'm not going to start thinking about *that.*

At nine o'clock Lisa hurried into Alida's office. "Oh, be still my heart," she whispered to Alida. "Paul-Anthony Payton is here for his appointment, and I have never in all my born days seen such a gorgeous man. He smiled at me, and it was all I could do to keep from tearing off my clothes and attacking his body."

Alida laughed. "Shame on you, Lisa Donovan."

"Can I have him for my birthday, Alida? Will you wrap him up, stick a big red bow on him, and give him to me so I can have my wicked way with him?"

"Certainly," Alida said. "In the meantime, would you please show Mr. Payton in?"

"Oh. Yes, I'd better do that. Some brazen hussy is liable to come along and snatch him right out of my office." Lisa rushed from the room.

Alida's smile faded, and she drew a steadying breath. Paul-Anthony Payton, she told herself, was a client of the Swan hotel. Nothing more. She was completely in control.

At that moment, Paul-Anthony strode into her office, smiling so intimately, heat poured through her lower body. "Hello, Alida."

No, she wasn't in control, Alida thought giddily as she got to her feet. If she was in complete control, why was her heart beating like a bongo drum? Why were her knees trembling?

"Good morning, Paul-Anthony," she said.

He closed the door and crossed the room.

"Please, sit down, won't you?" she said. "Would you care for a cup of coffee?" She settled back in her chair.

"No, thank you. I've had plenty of coffee already this morning." He sat down and placed his briefcase on the floor. "I love you, Alida."

Her eyes widened. "Would you stop saying that? For heaven's sake, what if someone hears you?"

He shrugged. "Then they'll know that I'm in love with you. The whole world is going to know eventually."

"They certainly are not."

"Sure they are, especially when we get married. I've made up my mind that I'm going to tell you that I love you every day of my life. I just took care of today's 'I love you, Alida.' "

"Paul-Anthony, you are sadly insane. Now, listen to me. As far as everyone here is concerned, we met in Max Brewer's office yesterday. You're here for the purpose, the sole purpose, of putting together your annual conference. Therefore, let's get to work. How many people are you expecting at your conference?"

"Lord, you're beautiful. I'd say about two hundred people. All of my top executives attend, as well as most of their spouses. You'll have your work cut out for you planning events for the spouses while the executives attend meetings. Fifteen of my executives are women, and some of them have husbands who come along." He sat back. "I think it's great that those men show support for their wives' careers. I will certainly respect your desire to work when we're married."

He paused. "Alida, put the paperweight down, okay? My nose has been broken twice, and I don't think it can go another round. It'll probably fall right off my face."

"Mr. Payton," Alida said, replacing the paperweight with a thud, "would you like fruit baskets in the attendees' rooms?"

"Great. Nice touch. Oh, and orchid corsages for the women the night of the final banquet. You have the most gorgeous strawberry-blond hair I've ever seen. I remember that it feels like silken threads when it's sliding through my fingers."

Alida cradled her head in her hands and groaned. "I'm not going to survive you."

Just love me, Paul-Anthony thought. Please.

Thank goodness it was Friday, Alida thought that evening as she walked down the hall to her apartment. She had the entire weekend to herself to relax and soothe her frazzled nerves. She was going to sleep, sleep, sleep.

"Pizza delivery," a voice called behind her.

She whirled around and stared at the man sauntering toward her. "Paul-Anthony! What are you doing here? How did you get past the security guard downstairs?"

"I'm here because you seem like a person who would enjoy a gooey pizza," he said, smiling. "As for the security guard . . ." He shrugged. "Chalk it up to my knock-'em-dead charm." And, he added silently, to the fact that the building's security system, including personnel, had been provided by Payton Security, aka John-Trevor Payton.

"I see," Alida said, glaring at him. She continued down the hall, then inserted her key in the door to her apartment.

Paul-Anthony inched the flat pizza box closer to her. "Double cheese, green peppers, black olives, pepperoni, sausage . . ."

Alida's stomach rumbled.

"Ah-ha!" he exclaimed. "I heard that. You, Miss Hunter, are hungry."

"You, Mr. Payton, are pushy."

"Hey, not me. I'm just being a nice guy, a thoughtful person. I intend to do nothing more than carry this pizza to your table, then leave."

"Oh," Alida said, opening the apartment door. That was *not* disappointment she was feeling. Of course she wanted him to leave. The last thing in the world she needed was Paul-Anthony spending the entire evening in her apartment. Just the two of them . . . together . . . For heaven's sake, no. "Well, fine," she said, stomping into the apartment. "I accept the pizza with my sincerest thanks."

She snapped on several lights as Paul-Anthony entered, shutting the door behind him.

"Hello, Scooter," she said as the cat bounded into the room. "Want some pizza?"

"Your cat likes pizza?" Paul-Anthony asked.

"He loves it."

"Weird."

Paul-Anthony crossed the living room and placed the box on the glass-top table in the dining alcove. Turning, he swept his gaze over the living room. The sofa and chairs were all soft curves and plump cushions, and she'd decorated in shades of pearl gray and brighter blues. "Nice place," he said. "It's very calming, peaceful." He lifted the lid of the box. "It's still warm. And it sure does smell good." He paused. "Well, enjoy."

Darn it, Alida thought. He was making her feel like the Wicked Witch of the West. There was enough pizza for her, Scooter, and ten of Scooter's friends. Oh, that Paul-Anthony Payton was a tricky son of a gun.

"All right," she said with a sigh, "you win. Would you care to stay and share the pizza?"

"No thanks," he said, starting toward the door.

"What?" She followed after him. "Why not? It's certainly big enough, and it was awfully nice of you to bring it. We can reheat it in the microwave to make it bubbly hot."

"Well—" He stopped with his hand on the doorknob. "I don't know. You already said I was pushy for showing up here in the first place."

"You took me by surprise. I'll go change my clothes, then we'll eat. Okay?"

"If you insist," he said, an expression of pure innocence on his face.

"I insist. I'll be right back."

Paul-Anthony watched her disappear down the hall, then grinned. "Score one for the good guys, Scooter," he said to the cat.

Alida put on jeans and a bright green T-shirt, then stepped into the bathroom to comb her hair. Frowning at her reflection, she replayed in her mind the conversation that had just taken place with Paul-Anthony.

That whole scene, she realized, had not gone well. Somehow, she'd ended up practically pleading with him to stay and share the pizza. How on earth had that happened?

Shaking her head in confusion, she headed for the kitchen. Paul-Anthony was taking a plate with several slices of pizza on it out of the microwave.

"First batch is hot," he said.

"I have some soda. Is that all right?"

"Sure. How much of this does Scooter get?"

"I'll give him a piece of my crust. Goodness, that smells better by the minute. I'm more hungry than I realized."

"Then let's dig in."

They sat across from each other at the dining table and, as Scooter gave serious attention to his piece of crust, they devoured the first slices without speaking. Paul-Anthony microwaved another plateful, then settled back into his chair.

"It's very apparent," he said, breaking the silence at last, "that you're good at your job. I was extremely impressed with your expertise today."

"Thank you. I enjoy what I do. Each new conference, meeting, no matter how big or small, is a challenge. Sometimes it gets so hectic I could scream, but for the most part it's very rewarding."

"I feel that way about my work too. However, I've come to realize that for too many years my entire life has been focused on my company. I intend to change that. But you know all this, don't you? We talked about it that night on the beach, the night of the fog."

The night their baby was conceived, Alida thought suddenly. No, no, she musn't think about the baby. Not when she was sitting across the table from Paul-Anthony.

"I'd appreciate it," she said, staring at the slice of pizza on her plate, "if you'd refrain from mentioning that night on the beach."

He reached across the table to take one of

her hands. "Why? It happened, Alida, and you know as well as I do that it was wonderful. I've also told you that I fell in love with you that night, deeply, irrevocably, forever in love with you."

"No." She attempted to free her hand, but he only tightened his hold. "I don't want you to be in love with me. It's pointless, and it will only cause you grief and pain. I don't intend to love again, Paul-Anthony, not ever." Except for their—*her* baby. "There are some people who are just not meant to fall in love, to have a conventional, committed relationship with another person, and I'm one of them."

"Alida—"

"You, Paul Anthony, *want* to be in love and get married. Don't make the same mistake I did. Don't choose the wrong person and end up with a broken heart and shattered dreams. I *am* the wrong woman, and the sooner you accept that, the better. Move on, Paul-Anthony, look for her somewhere else. She's out there. You simply haven't found her yet."

Yes, he had, Paul-Anthony thought fiercely. She was sitting across from him at that very moment. Lord, what was it going to take for him to get through to Alida? He had to be patient. His entire future happiness was centered on winning her love. And he would do it. Because she was his.

He released her hand and glanced at the cardboard box. "Want me to heat up some more pizza?"

"No, I've had plenty. Paul-Anthony, did you hear what I said? Were you listening to me?"

"I heard you. Can Scooter have this little piece of crust?"

She sighed. "Yes, go ahead and give it to him."

"I'm not that crazy about cats, but Scooter has really got personality. The fact that he likes pizza is a point in his favor. He's a great cat."

"And you," Alida said, getting to her feet, "are an exasperating man. Would you care for some chocolate ice cream?"

"Perfect."

Remaining seated at the table, he watched her walk into the kitchen and retrieve a tub of ice cream from the freezer. She was so beautiful, he mused. And for the first time since his adolescence, he was the pursuer instead of the pursued. All of his adult life he, as well as his brothers, had been sought out by women who made it clear they liked what they saw and were available for the asking. The Payton boys had always had the pick of the cream of the crop.

Well, he thought dryly, he was getting his comeuppance now. He was in love for the first time in his life, and the lady wanted no part of him. Talk about eating humble pie.

Alida was rejecting him at every turn. But what she didn't know was that the Payton brothers had received more than just their names from their feisty French mother. They'd also inherited her stubbornness and determination. He just wished their *maman* had tossed in a hefty dose of patience.

"Ice cream," Alida said, returning to the table and plunking a bowl in front of him. She sat down, then yawned hugely. "My, I'm just exhausted after such an extremely busy week."

Paul-Anthony suppressed a smile as he swallowed a spoonful of ice cream. Oh, yes, he thought, he definitely had his work cut out for him.

As they ate their dessert in silence, Alida couldn't resist stealing glances at Paul-Anthony from beneath her lashes. All the time they'd been eating their pizza, and even when she'd been in the kitchen, she'd felt a strange, crackling tension building between them, a sensual awareness that grew with every beat of her racing heart. He had to get out of there, she thought frantically, before she did something she would regret.

I love you, Alida Hunter.

Never again, she vowed, would she fall prey to those words. She'd fixed her focus on her baby, and the life they would have together. She no longer considered her actions that night on the beach shameful. No, it had been a magical time that had resulted in the precious miracle nestled deep within her. That Paul-Anthony Payton had been the man in the mist *meant nothing.*

"Finished?" he asked, peering into her bowl. "I'll wash these up."

"No need." She stood and snatched his bowl. "I'll put them in the dishwasher. Thank you for the pizza. I enjoyed it, but as I said, I'm exhausted."

"Then I'd better be on my way so you can get some sleep."

He stood up, and she set the bowls back onto the table. "I'll see you to the door."

Paul-Anthony wandered into the living room with Alida right behind him. She went to the door, but he moved in the opposite direction to study the books that filled a large bookcase.

"Yes," he said, nodding. "These are the books you told me about that night on the beach." He turned to face her, his expression serious. "But then, everything we said that night was the truth, spoken from our hearts, openly and honestly. Right, Alida?"

She remained by the door, forcing herself to stand straight and stiff. "Don't, Paul-Anthony. There's nothing to be accomplished by continually referring to that night. I wish you'd accept things the way they are."

"I have, Alida. I certainly have." He walked

slowly toward her. "I've accepted that I fell deeply in love with you then. I've accepted that I told you my intermost secrets, doubts, fears, hopes, and dreams, and you shared yours with me. I've accepted that you're afraid to love, to trust in your own judgment, and I'm mustering every ounce of patience I have to give you time to learn that you can believe in me."

He stopped directly in front of her, only inches away. Alida backed up, but the door halted her retreat. Paul-Anthony braced his hands on the door, on either side of her head, and moved closer yet, his body not quite touching hers.

He held her gaze, and heated passion began to swirl deep within her. She drew in a shaky breath, and the tantalizing scent of his aftershave filled her senses. She recognized the desire radiating from his eyes—and she remembered the night in the mist with almost painful clarity.

"No," she whispered, her voice and knees trembling. "I don't want . . ."

"Me?" He lowered his head toward hers. "Are you so very certain of that?" He brushed his lips over hers. She shivered. "Are you, Alida? Don't you want to make love with me again, feel me inside you as we become one? It was so beautiful"—he outlined her lips with the tip of his tongue—"so incredibly beautiful."

His mouth melted over hers, his tongue delving between her lips to find hers. A soft sob caught in Alida's throat as she savored the taste, the feel, the wondrous sensation of Paul-Anthony's kiss.

Weaving his fingers through her hair, he closed the remaining distance between them. His body molded to hers, his arousal heavy and hard against her. She circled his neck with her arms and drank of him, filling herself with the essence of Paul-Anthony Payton.

Paul-Anthony struggled to hang on to his control as he felt Alida surrendering, giving way to the desire within her. Lord he wanted her. He'd ached for her ever since she'd run from him, disappearing into the fog.

Yet he knew, despite his raging passion, that making love with Alida that night would be wrong. Yes, she was surrendering, but it wasn't enough.

Though their bodies would join in wondrous ecstasy, he would not have touched her heart, her soul. The burning ache in his body would be appeased, but Alida would still be as elusive as the mist on the beach.

He gathered his restraint, envisioning it as a strong fist pushing him away from the woman he loved. He tore his lips from Alida's and stepped back, drawing a shuddering breath.

Alida opened her eyes. A chill swept through

her as she instantly missed the heat of Paul-Anthony's body. Her breasts were heavy, sensitive, craving a soothing touch. Her blood hummed in her veins, and an insistent message of want and need pulsed low within her.

His hands shaking, Paul-Anthony gently grasped her upper arms and moved her away from the door. She stared at him, unable to think, hardly able to breathe.

"Good night, Alida." he said, his voice rough with surpressed passion. "I love you, and I love you. That covers Saturday and Sunday. I'll see you next week."

"I—" Alida started, then stopped, realizing she had no sensible thought in her head.

He gripped the doorknob. "I could have made love to you tonight, Alida. I know it and you know it. But I want, and intend to have, more than just your body. I want all of you. Your heart, your trust, your love. That's it, bottom line. I want your love forever. You're mine. You have been since the night in the mist. You'll have the time you need to sort it through, but I'll be close, very close, to remind you that this is real, that this is forever."

And then he was gone with a quiet click of the closing door.

Alida blinked. She stood motionless for a minute, then made her way to the sofa and sank onto it.

She would have done it, she thought in

astonishment. She would have made love with Paul-Anthony. She'd wanted him so very much, and just like that night on the beach, it had seemed right that she give herself to him, become one with him.

When he touched her, kissed her, reason fled along with reality. He swept her away on a tide of desire, until she was aware of only her yearning for their exquisite lovemaking.

He was dangerous. Paul-Anthony Payton had a strange hold on her. There, in her own apartment, he'd become once again the man of the mist. He had just melded that night into this night—intertwining what she struggled to keep apart.

It mustn't happen again.

She had to be stronger, resist him until he tired of continuous defeat and moved on. She would not make love with him because, she knew, she'd then risk falling in love with him.

To love was to lose. To love was to cry tears of heartache and suffer the chill of loneliness.

She rested her hands on her stomach and closed her eyes. Centering her thoughts on the baby within her, she forced Paul-Anthony Payton farther and farther away, until he was consumed by a mist . . . and disappeared.

Three

Much to Alida's delight, the weekend was filled with pleasurable hours. She cleaned her apartment, shopped for groceries, and treated herself to a new book she'd been eager to read.

She spoke on the telephone to Dr. Allen on Saturday morning, and assured the doctor that all was well. She was happy about the baby, but could live without the morning sickness that plagued her at dawn. Dr. Allen recommended she keep soda crackers on her nightstand to munch on before she got up.

"I'll want to see you in a month," the doctor added. "In the meantime . . . have you given thought to telling the father about the baby?"

"Yes," Alida said, "and he's not going to be told. I know what you said—it's his child too—but the circumstances are such that it isn't really his because— Oh, it's just too complicated to explain. These are the nineties, Dr. Allen. There's no stigma attached to being an unwed mother, a single parent. The baby and I will do fine. We'll have each other, love each other."

"It won't be easy, Alida. Being a single parent is a tremendous undertaking. But it's your decision. Remember to eat balanced meals, don't get overtired, and I'll see you in a month."

"Thank you and, believe me, I intend to take very good care of myself and my precious cargo. Good-bye."

With a smile firmly in place, Alida hung up and walked into the spare bedroom. It was empty, except for several boxes of odds and ends shoved into one corner. She mentally decorated the room, turning it into an enchanting nursery done in pale yellow and mint green.

On Sunday afternoon she wandered leisurely through the baby department of a large store, her heart quickening with excitement as she fingered the incredibly small clothes. On impulse, she bought a delicate crocheted blanket with a matching sweater, booties, and cap.

Back in the apartment, she gazed tenderly at the whisper-soft garments, then brushed the tissue back over them, covered the box, and placed it carefully on the closet shelf in the soon-to-be nursery.

Before drifting off to sleep Sunday night, Alida told herself that it was understandable and unimportant that Paul-Anthony Payton had hovered in the back of her mind during the entire weekend. He was, after all, a client of the Swan Hotel, and, she reassured herself, she *had* also thought about the approaching writers' conference.

No, there was nothing threatening, she reasoned, about Paul-Anthony being in her thoughts. She was fully in charge of her emotions, her life, everything.

The soda crackers helped immensely Monday morning, and Alida felt well rested and cheerful when she entered her office. Jerry was perched on the edge of Lisa's desk, talking to the secretary.

"Good morning," Alida said.

"Good-bye," Lisa said to Jerry, glaring at the handsome man. "Get your tush off my desk."

Jerry stood and chuckled. "You'd better work on your attitude, honey. You'll never snag a man by being a shrew." He shifted his gaze to Alida. "Unless, of course, you intend to be a liberated career woman like our boss here."

Alida frowned. "What's wrong with you?"

He shook his head. "Nothing. Look, I'm sorry, okay? I'm in a lousy mood because I've got the worst hangover of my entire life. I'll see you later."

Alida watched him stride out of the office, then glanced at Lisa. "I've never seen him act like that. What was he saying to you when I came in?"

"The jerk asked me out to dinner, making it clear that dessert would be going to bed with him. Oh, lucky me. I swear, some men are so disgusting. Not all men, you understand, but some . . . a lot. The majority of the species, in fact." She tapped one fingertip against her chin. "Now, if Paul-Anthony Payton had made me the same offer, that would be another story. Drat. He doesn't have an appointment with you until Thursday."

Thank goodness for that, Alida thought as she went into her office.

The morning was busy. Alida met with the head of housekeeping to discuss the color scheme for the writers' awards banquet. The conference coordinator had requested burgundy and pink, and had told Alida the table centerpieces would be furnished by one of the conference committees. Alida jotted a note to herself to ask Paul-Anthony what color scheme he preferred for the banquet for his group.

She then met with the engineer of the hotel about spotlights during the awards presentation at the writers' banquet. Another note joined the growing list of things to ask Paul-Anthony.

Paul-Anthony, Alida realized as she ate her lunch at her desk, was creeping into every area of her job. But that was understandable. Of course it was. She was putting together a conference for the man, for heaven's sake. She had to discuss a multitude of details with him. No problem. It was strictly business.

At two o'clock in the afternoon Lisa breezed into Alida's office, carrying a crystal bud vase. It contained a single deep red rose. A matching velvet bow was tied around the delicate vase.

"For you," Lisa said, beaming as she put the vase on the desk. "It was just delivered. The card is there. See? It's tucked under the ribbon."

Alida stared at the flower. "Yes, I see it."

"So? Aren't you going to open the card?"

"No. Well, yes, but . . ."

"I can take a hint. Brother, you're no fun." Lisa spun around and left the office.

Alida narrowed her eyes, as though by doing so she could read the card inside the small envelope. With a sigh of defeat she slid the envelope free of the ribbon and slowly pulled out the card. As she read the words written in a bold, sprawling handwriting, the beat of her racing heart thundered in her ears.

I said I'd say it every day, the message read. *I love you, Alida. Paul-Anthony.*

"Oh, damn, damn," she whispered.

She started to tear the card in two, but hesitated. Of their own volition, it seemed, her hands slid the card back into the envelope, then tucked it into her purse. She glared at the rose, which was already enchanting her with its lovely aroma, and shifted the vase to the edge of the desk.

During the remainder of the day her gaze was drawn time and again to the exquisite flower.

Tuesday's rose was yellow, the exact shade, Alida realized, as the crocheted outfit she'd purchased for the baby. No, it wasn't. No, it wasn't! She would not allow Paul-Anthony to move into the private space where the existence of her child was carefully hidden.

Wednesday's rose was pure white, like the fog on the beach. Enough was enough, Alida thought, scowling at the flower. With each rose had been a card with the message, *I love you, Alida.* Paul-Anthony was carrying out his threat—promise?—to declare his love for her every day. And he was driving her crazy, rubbing her nerves raw. She would see him the next day when he came in for his appointment, and she would tell him that he was—

"Sooo romantic," Lisa said, coming into Alida's office. "You should take the roses home, Alida, so you can enjoy them in the evening."

"No," Alida said quickly. "They don't belong there, in my home. What I mean is . . . Never mind."

Lisa placed several papers on Alida's desk. "These letters are ready for your signature." She ran one fingertip over a velvety petal of the yellow rose, then glanced at Alida. "You're being so secretive about who sent the roses. You and I have been friends for several years now, Alida, and . . . I don't know. I guess I feel as though you've drawn a line between us, made it clear that you're the boss and I'm the secretary, and you don't share your personal business with the hired help. I'm sorry if that sounds childish, but . . ." She shrugged.

"Oh, Lisa," Alida said, "we *are* friends, always will be. Think about all the dinners we've shared, the movies and concerts we've gone to together. The shopping sprees. I'm sorry if I've hurt your feelings by not telling you who sent the roses. I just can't because it's a very complicated situation and— Please, don't let my silence tarnish our friendship."

"Oh, Lord, Alida, you're not involved with a married man, are you? Is that why you can't tell me who he is?"

"No, he isn't married. Lisa, I'm not really involved with anyone."

Lisa's gaze swept over the three bud vases. "Right," she said dryly. "Well, I won't ask again about the roses. I really am acting silly and immature, but I thought we were such close friends and . . ." She threw up her hands. "Forget it. I sound like a little girl." She turned and hurried out of the office.

"Lisa . . ." Alida started out of her chair, then sank back down. She'd hurt Lisa's feelings terribly, but there was no sense in going after her to explain about who'd sent the roses. She couldn't. Oh, for two cents she'd strangle Paul-Anthony Payton with her bare hands.

"Tomorrow, Mr. Payton, you're going to get a hefty piece of my mind."

Late the next afternoon Paul-Anthony strode across the large parking lot of the Swan Hotel.

In a few minutes he'd see Alida. His Alida. Beautiful Alida. The roses and the messages on each card had been genius-level brain work, he complimented himself. There was no doubt in his mind that he'd kept himself in Alida's thoughts since the last time he'd seen her.

Flowers always made a hit with women. He'd pictured her smiling winsomely as she gazed at the roses. She'd read and reread the cards, realizing he had meant it when he'd said he'd declare his love for her every day.

Oh, yes, he thought smugly, nodding at

the uniformed man who opened the door for him, he was making great progress. In just moments, Alida's face would light up with happiness when she saw him enter her office. Go for it, Payton. He was on a roll.

"Paul-Anthony Payton is here," Lisa said to Alida. "And he's as gorgeous as ever," she added *sotto voce*. "Dark suit with a pale gray shirt and dark tie, and it's a knockout combination with his coloring. He really is scrumptious. Shall I show him in?"

"Please do," Alida said, getting to her feet. Lisa was pleasant but subdued, she noted. Alida could only hope there hadn't been permanent damage to their friendship. "Please hold my calls, Lisa."

"Sure."

As Lisa left the room, Alida smoothed the waistband of the lightweight pale blue sweater she wore over a navy blue skirt. She quickly slipped on the tailored jacket, deciding that since she was wearing a power suit, she would act accordingly. The fact that the button on her skirt was undone and her waistline now made it necessary to leave the zipper open an inch or so was irrelevant. She was ready for battle with Mr. Paul-Anthony Payton.

"Hello, Alida," Paul-Anthony said, smiling as he closed the office door behind him. His gaze flickered over the three bud vases on her desk. There they are, he thought. Sitting on her desk and not in the trash. He was doing well. And Alida was even coming out from behind her desk to greet him. "I love you on this Thursday, Alida Hunter."

"This," she said tightly, marching right up to him, "could very well be the last Thursday you'll draw breath, Mr. Payton. You are a dead man."

"Huh?"

"You are the most arrogant so-and-so I've ever had the unfortunate fate to meet." She punctuated her words by poking his chest with one finger. "If it weren't for the fact that you're not worth going to jail for, I'd gladly murder you."

"What?" he said incredulously. This, he realized, was *not* going well. Dammit, what had gone wrong? "You don't like roses?"

"I don't like *you!*" Oh, darn it, Alida thought. Why did he have to smell so good, and look so good, and cause her to remember . . . Alida, shut up. "You're disrupting my life, causing me immeasurable problems, and I want it stopped this very instant. I'm sure you're accustomed to having your way with women, Mr. Payton, but not this time. You'll either agree to conduct yourself in a strictly businesslike manner with me, or the planning of your conference will be handled by my assistant, Jerry Nash."

Paul-Anthony ran one hand over the back of his neck. "Oh," he said quietly. "Well, that's certainly clear enough, isn't it?"

She had not, Alida told herself, seen a flicker of hurt in Paul-Anthony's compelling blue eyes. He was intrigued by her, had convinced himself he loved her, but that emotion was fleeting. It would fade away, just like the mist on the beach. Just like the declarations of love she'd heard in the past. In the meantime, he had to leave her alone.

She lifted her chin. "I'm glad we understand each other at last. Are you ready to discuss the conference? I have a long list of details to go over with you."

"Fine," Paul-Anthony said. Dammit, he thought. Now what did he do? He'd been so certain that the roses would soften her, but he was back to square one. Hell, he was minus square one. This pursuer business was a lot tougher than he'd thought. Okay, so he'd have to regroup. But for now, he supposed, he'd concentrate on the damnable conference. "Shall we sit down?"

That was it? Alida wondered. Just "Shall we sit down?" No argument, no further declarations of love, no reminders of what they'd shared that foggy night on the beach?

"Yes, of course," she said, spinning around. "We—we shall sit down." She strode behind her desk and sank gratefully into her chair, only then realizing how badly her legs were trembling.

Paul-Anthony sat opposite her, placed his briefcase on the edge of the desk, and flipped open the latches. He removed a file, closed the briefcase, then settled back in his chair, his face expressionless.

What was he up to? Alida wondered.

She fiddled with some papers on her desk, stealing a quick glance at him.

Oh, now, wait a minute, she thought. Paul-Anthony was being tricky again. The night he'd showed up at her apartment with the pizza, he'd somehow turned things around so that she nearly pleaded with him to stay and share the dinner.

His calm "Shall we sit down?" had been intended to throw her off balance—which it had. But she had his number now; she was a step beyond Mr. Payton's cleverness. She was in total control of the situation. She hoped.

They worked steadily for the next hour, covering the many details Alida had listed to go over with him. As she checked off each item, she dismally admitted to herself that her heart was beating too fast, that a curling warmth was pulsing deep within her, that she was acutely aware of every magnificent, masculine inch of Paul-Anthony Payton.

At five o'clock Lisa knocked lightly on the door, poked her head in the room, and said good night.

"Oh, yes, good night, Lisa," Alida said. "Have a nice evening."

"See you tomorrow." Lisa stared at the back of Paul-Anthony, rolled her eyes heavenward in appreciation, then disappeared, closing the door again.

Another half hour passed.

"That covers it for now," Alida said finally. "If your secretary gets the invitations out next week and includes the hotel registration form, we'll be on our way. I've put a tentative block on the number of rooms you'll need, but the sooner the registration forms come in, the better. Then I can release the rooms that aren't needed for general use. If your secretary states in the letter the cutoff date for registration, and that it's firm, it will help immensely."

"Fine," Paul-Anthony said. "And you'll talk to the hotel concierge about day excursions for the spouses?"

"Yes. I'll have a list for you to examine when we meet again next week."

"Excellent." He replaced the file in his briefcase and stood up. "As I said before, you're very good at what you do, Alida. I'm extremely impressed."

"Thank you." She stood and walked around the desk. "I'll see you out and— Oh. Oh, dear."

A wave of dizziness swept over her with strange black dots dancing wildly before her eyes. A rushing noise echoed in her ears. She reached out blindly for the edge of the desk, the floor seeming to tilt as though rushing up to meet her.

Then everything went black.

"Okay, Alida," a soothing voice said, "you've been fading in and out on me long enough. It's time to come all the way back and let me officially introduce myself."

Forget it, Alida thought foggily. She was too tired to open her eyes. Besides, she was so comfortable snuggled in her bed, and whoever this yo-yo was who wanted to introduce himself, he could just go away. Oh, good Lord, why was there a strange man in her bedroom?

Her eyes popped open and she found herself staring at a little roly-poly man with snow white hair and a fluffy beard.

"Santa Claus?" she asked weakly.

The man chuckled. "I've been told for years that I look like the old boy, but I'm Dr. Hans Nelson. You're on the sofa in your secretary's office, Alida. You fainted, Paul-Anthony called me, and you've been in and out on me for about twenty minutes."

"Oh. Paul-Anthony called you?"

"I'm retired now, but I was the Payton boys' doctor from the time they were born. Rough-necks, every one of them. I consider it a major accomplishment of my career to have kept them patched together all those years."

"I . . ."

"Paul-Anthony is out in the corridor pacing like a caged animal. He was a wreck by the time I got here, and was more trouble than he was worth. I threatened to break his nose if he didn't keep out of my way."

"His nose has been broken twice already." Oh, what a stupid thing to say, she thought.

"I know. I was the one who tended to it both times. Now, young lady, let's concentrate on you. My eagle eye and sixth sense tells me what your condition is, but let's chat a bit, shall we?"

Paul-Anthony halted in front of the closed door and reached for the door knob, then swore as he pulled back his hand.

Five more minutes, he told himself, resuming his pacing. That was the longest he would wait before going into that office. Alida had fainted right into his arms! She'd been so still, so pale, and he'd been scared out of his mind.

What was wrong with Alida, his beautiful Alida? He needed to see her, to touch her and be assured that she was all right. He'd never felt so helpless in his entire life. And now he'd been banished to the hallway like a naughty kid by that damnable Dr. Nelson. Five more minutes, maximum.

The door to the office opened, and Dr. Nelson stepped out, closing the door behind him. Paul-Anthony spun around and covered the distance between them in two long, heavy strides.

"Well?" he asked. "Is she okay? What's wrong with her? Why did she faint? She was as pale as a ghost and . . . Come on, Doc, talk to me."

Dr. Nelson frowned and ran one hand down his beard. "Why do you want to know all this? What is Alida Hunter to you, Paul-Anthony?"

"I'm in love with her. I'm going to marry her, spend the rest of my life with her."

"I see," Dr. Nelson said. "That's good news. When are you planning on marrying her?"

"Just as soon as I can convince her that *she's* in love with *me.* I'm running into a bit of a problem with that part, but I'll win. I have to. I've waited a lifetime for Alida, and I don't intend to lose her. Forget what I just said. What's wrong with her?"

"Alida was not forthcoming with information. I had to present to her facts that she couldn't deny. When I mentioned your name at that point, however, she refused to utter another word. To say you have a bit of a problem regarding her feelings for you is, I think, putting it mildly."

"I know," Paul-Anthony said quietly. "She

doesn't want to be in love. She was badly hurt by a self-centered mother, and the man she was engaged to betrayed her. Alida's determined never to love again. She's decided she's not meant to love . . . ever. But, Doc, she's my life. I love her and I need her. I've been alone and lonely so damn long. Please, tell me why she fainted. If she's sick, I'll get her the best medical care in the country."

"She's not ill," Dr. Nelson said. "Let me see here. There is a code, you know, of doctor and patient confidentiality. But I'm not her doctor. I am, in fact, retired, a simple citizen, whom you happened to call when the young lady fainted. If I turn out to be a blabbermouth, shame on me, But I'm *not* Alida Hunter's physician."

"Doc, what are you blithering about? I'm going in there to see for myself that Alida is all right."

"Don't you move, Paul-Anthony. I have to sort this through."

"Well, hell, can't you sort a little faster? I'm worried out of my mind, Doc."

"Yes, I can see that. You're very much in love with Alida. Your dear mother would be delighted. Your dear mother would also skin you alive if you didn't do the proper thing under these circumstances, but from what you've said, you want to marry Alida."

"Yes, I do. But she's fighting me every inch of the way."

"I suggest you fight back with a lot more vigor, my boy."

"Doc, you're confusing the hell out of me. You're not making an awful lot of sense, and you still haven't told me what's wrong with Alida."

"Paul-Anthony, am I to assume you and Alida have made love?"

"For crying out loud, Doc, that's none of your business."

"Answer the question."

"Dammit, yes, we've made love. Okay? Satisfied? Why are you capable of intimidating me now the same way you could when I was a kid?"

"Because I'm a mean old man. Well, rationalizing that I can divulge this information because I'm no longer a practicing physician, and taking into consideration the fact that I adored your mother, and you boys, for more years than I—"

"Doc," Paul-Anthony said, through clenched teeth, "I'm going into that room."

"All right, Paul-Anthony. But you'd better hear the truth first. That young woman is pregnant. It would seem, my boy, Alida Hunter is carrying your baby."

Four

Paul-Anthony was vaguely aware of thanking Dr. Nelson for coming to the hotel so quickly, then bidding him good-bye. When the old doctor hesitated and asked if he was all right, Paul-Anthony mumbled a less-than-intelligent something about being just dandy. Dr. Nelson chuckled, shook his head, then shuffled off down the hall.

Paul-Anthony stood frozen outside the office door, emotions tumbling together with such speed, he was unable to deal with one before the next slammed into place.

And echoing over and over, like the pounding of an insistent drummer, was the incredible, nearly unbelievable message of truth.

Alida Hunter was pregnant with his baby.

He dragged his shaking hands down his face, then drew in a deep breath. A baby, he thought. His baby, his and Alida's.

It was wonderful, fantastic. The woman he loved was going to have his child.

But she hadn't told him. She knew she was pregnant. She'd had to know even before Dr. Nelson figured it out. Weeks and weeks had passed since that foggy night . . . Oh, yes, Alida knew.

Paul-Anthony narrowed his eyes. Dammit, Alida had had no intention of telling him about the baby, his baby. She was doing everything within her power to keep him at arm's length, to hold fast to her vow never to love again, to hide behind the walls she'd built around her heart.

She'd planned on keeping him from knowing about his own child! How could she even consider doing such a thing?

Because she was frightened, a small voice in his mind whispered. Because she didn't believe in his declarations of love for her, didn't believe in *him.* She'd been hurt in the past, and he was picking up the tab, paying the price for things he hadn't done.

But, dear Lord, that was his baby, *their* baby, and the knowledge that he might never have known about his own child was chilling, Alida's silence cutting him like the vicious, gleaming blade of a knife.

He wanted to roar in anger.

He wanted to gather Alida into his arms, tell her she wasn't alone, that he was ecstatic about the baby, that they'd be married immediately.

He wanted to rage in fury, make her feel the same excruciating pain he'd experienced as he'd realized she would have kept his child from him.

He wanted to hold her tightly and never, ever let her go.

Exhausted by the emotions whipping through him, Paul-Anthony slumped against the door. He was a wreck. He didn't know what to do, or say, or think. But nothing was going to be accomplished by standing out in the corridor.

After taking another steadying breath, he entered the office.

Alida got to her feet the instant Paul-Anthony appeared. She searched his face for some clue as to what was going on in his mind but found only an unreadable expression.

Did he know about the baby? she wondered. Had Dr. Nelson told him? No, surely not, because doctors weren't allowed to divulge what their patients told them. But she wasn't Dr. Nelson's patient. He was a retired doctor as well as a long-standing friend of the Payton family. Oh, dear heaven, did Paul-Anthony know she was carrying his child?

"I'm sorry for all the fuss," she said unsteadily. "I must have forgotten to eat lunch today and— But I'm fine now, and I thank you for calling the doctor, although it wasn't necessary. Your briefcase, I assume, is still in my office. So, if you'll get it, I'll lock up and be on my way. I do appreciate your—"

"I'm taking you home," he interrupted quietly.

"Oh, no, there's no need for that. I'm perfectly capable of getting home on my own. Besides, I have my car here."

"I'll see that it's driven to your apartment. I'm taking you home, Alida."

She frowned. Paul-Anthony appeared calm enough, but there was an underlying something to his manner that she couldn't define. He was speaking softly, yet there was a steely edge to his voice that indicated he wouldn't stand for any argument.

"Well . . ." she began.

"Lock up." He strode into her office and returned with his briefcase. "Lock up, Alida, and let's go."

Good idea, she thought, turning to her office. She was still slightly lightheaded, and was not up to a major confrontation with Paul-Anthony regarding transportation. So he would take her home, she'd thank him politely for his efforts on her behalf, and that would be that.

Unless . . .

Oh, dear Lord, *did* Paul-Anthony know about the baby?

"All right, Paul-Anthony," she said as she stepped out of her office and locked the door behind her. "I accept your offer of a ride home. My car will be safe here overnight, and I'll take a taxi in the morning."

He didn't reply, and she eyed him warily as they left the hotel. His silver BMW was new, plush, and smelled deliciously of fine leather. The drive to her apartment was made in total silence.

"You can just drop me off," she said as they approached her building.

"I'll see you in."

Okay, she thought rather giddily. Paul-Anthony wanted to deposit her safely inside her apartment? Then, by golly, that's what he'd do. She'd bid him a pleasant adieu, close the door, and have a nervous breakdown. He was just so damnably quiet, it was giving her the crazies.

Silence again hung heavily in the air as they rode up in the elevator and walked down the corridor to her apartment. She flicked on the lights, forced a smile onto her face, and turned to look at what she assumed would be her immediately-exiting escort.

But Paul-Anthony had shrugged out of his suit coat and was striding past her, heading for the kitchen.

She spun around and planted her fists on her hips. "Excuse me, Mr. Payton, but just what do you think you're doing?"

He stopped at the kitchen doorway and looked at her. "Making us some dinner. Go change into something comfortable."

"I certainly will not."

He shrugged. "Then stay in your I'm-a-big-cheese suit, I don't care. I'm still going to fix some food."

She glanced down at her severely tailored outfit. "What's wrong with this suit?" she muttered. "I'm-a-big-cheese suit? That's rude. That is very, very rude."

She marched into the kitchen to find Paul-Anthony peering into the refrigerator.

"Now, you listen," she said. "You can't come waltzing in here and take over as though you own the place. This my apartment and— Yes, those are my eggs you just took out of my refrigerator, and— Oh, hi, Scooter," she interrupted herself as the cat appeared. "And this is my cat and . . . Paul-Anthony Payton, go home."

He straightened and looked at her with an expression so intense, yet still so totally undefinable, a shiver coursed through her.

"Alida," he said, his voice ominously low, "I'm going to prepare scrambled eggs and toast, which will be a good trick because I've never made scrambled eggs before in my life.

We are going to eat scrambled eggs and toast. And then we're going to have a serious discussion. I suggest that you feed your cat and change your clothes." He paused. "Now."

She stared at him, wide-eyed. "Yes . . . well, I . . ."

"Right now."

"Got it."

Scooter was fed, then Alida changed into jeans, the waistband of which she could no longer button, a fact she hid with a baggy gray sweatshirt. She delayed her return to the kitchen as long as possible.

"Alida!" Paul-Anthony finally yelled.

Dragging her feet, she headed toward the dining alcove. Actually, she wanted to go in the opposite direction.

He was acting so strangely, she mused, and the situation was quite obviously out of her control. Even more, she still didn't know if Dr. Nelson had told him about the baby. He wanted to have a serious discussion? Oh, mercy, about what?

"The eggs, such as they are," Paul-Anthony said, "are ready. They're a bit hard, but . . ."

She slid onto her chair, and he plunked a glass of milk down by her plate. Milk? Milk! Was that a subtle clue, a warning that he knew about—

He set a glass of milk by his own plate, then sat down. "I couldn't figure out how to stir the eggs, make toast, *and* fix coffee," he said. "So we're having milk. Eat."

Cancel the clue, Alida thought. Some detective she was. Damn, she was getting hysterical. And these were, without a doubt, the worst scrambled eggs she'd ever had the misfortune to eat.

They didn't speak for several minutes.

"Alida," Paul-Anthony finally said, breaking the silence.

"What!" she yelled, nearly jumping out of her chair.

"If you sneak one more bite of eggs to Scooter, I'm going to shut him in the bedroom. This is a crummy dinner, but that's the breaks. Eat."

"You," she said, leaning toward him, "are a very rude person."

"Because you," he said, matching her glare, "have pushed me to the limit of my patience." He looked down at his plate. "Lord, this is disgusting. Forget dinner. Let's go into the living room."

Oh, let's not, Alida thought. She felt trapped, cornered, like a frightened kitten. She walked on trembling legs into the living room, and sat on the sofa. Paul-Anthony roamed around the room, then stopped in front of the bookcase, his back to her.

"Is there anything you'd care to tell me?" he asked quietly.

She drew a steadying breath. "Tell you? Are we chatting? Well, you're a lousy cook."

Don't, Alida, Paul-Anthony thought. He wanted so much for her to tell him about the baby, to share the glorious news that their lovemaking had created a new life, a miracle. But she wasn't going to do it. And, damn, it hurt.

He turned to face her. "I know about the baby."

Oh, dear heaven, Alida thought. Paul-Anthony Payton spoke five words and her world came crashing down. Five little words.

I know about the baby.

No, no, no, she cried silently. He was invading her safe, protected world where all of her love would be centered on her child. He didn't belong there because he was dangerous. He caused desire to swell within her, and her heart to wish that this magnificent man could love her for all time. But that kind of love was just beyond her reach, not hers to have.

I know about the baby.

She lifted her chin and willed herself not to cry. Gathering every ounce of courage she could muster, she spoke in a voice she prayed was steady.

"I see. Well, it really doesn't matter because— because there's a good chance that . . . it isn't yours."

Paul-Anthony stiffened, as though he'd just been brutally punched in the gut. "What?"

"Think about it, Paul-Anthony," she said, picking an imaginary thread from her jeans. "I told you that Carl had come back after being away all those months. Granted, he told me he'd fallen in love with another woman. But before he confessed that little news flash we . . ." She shrugged. "I don't believe details are necessary." Lies, such hideous lies, but she was desperate. She had no choice but to do it this way. "The baby is mine. Who its father is is immaterial. So I'm sure you'll agree that under the circumstances, there's no point in pursuing this serious discussion of yours further. Good-bye."

He stared at her. Seconds ticked by. Silence hovered over them like a nearly tangible entity. The seconds turned into minutes.

"Alida . . ." he said finally.

She met his gaze.

"I don't believe you."

"You what?"

"No, it doesn't work, not for a minute. Carl, when you analyze it, handled the situation with at least a bit of class. He fell in love with someone else, betrayed you in a sense, but those things do happen. He didn't just disappear. He didn't write you a Dear Jane letter. He didn't tell you on the phone. No, he waited until he could tell you face-to-face. So, okay, you chose the wrong man, but he had the decency to confront you in person. You didn't make love with him that day. He wouldn't have done it because it doesn't fit the picture of the way he conducted himself."

"I . . ."

"Alida, that baby is mine. The child was conceived that night on the beach, during the most incredibly beautiful lovemaking I've ever experienced. I'm that baby's father."

Alida dropped her face into her hands, fighting against the emotions and tears threatening to overcome her. She was suddenly so exhausted, it was an effort to breathe and beyond her to think.

Everything was coming apart at once, and she didn't know where to put it all, how to handle it. She wanted to crawl into bed, pull the blankets over her head, and sleep. Just sleep.

Paul-Anthony hunkered down in front of her and gently pulled her hands from her face. "Look at me."

She shook her head.

"Alida, please, look at me."

She slowly raised her head to meet his gaze.

"Alida, don't you see? You're not alone, it isn't just *your* baby. It's *our* baby, a tiny person who will be a blend of you and me, but an individual in his own right. I want our baby more than I can tell you, and I want—I *need*, you in my life forever. Alida Hunter, I love you very much. So very much."

That did it.

Alida lost her battle against the myriad of emotions, and after one wobbly sob she burst into tears.

Frowning, Paul-Anthony straightened and reached into his back pocket for a pristine white handkerchief. He pressed it into her hands, then sat down next to her on the sofa, circling her shoulders with one arm.

"Don't cry," he said, then paused. "No, wait. Maybe you should cry. Yes, have a good old-fashioned cry, the kind men have envied from the beginning of time."

"No, tears won't help," Alida said, dabbing at her nose with a handkerchief. "Everything just caught up with me, that's all." She sniffled. "I had it all worked out, knew exactly what I was going to do, but then . . ." She shook her head.

"Then," he said, his jaw tightening, "I found out about *our* baby. I'm having a hard time accepting the fact you weren't going to tell me about my own child! But that's behind us now, because I do know, and everything is going to be fine. We'll be married immediately and—"

Her head snapped up. "No. I'm not going to marry you."

"Dammit, Alida," he said, his voice rising.

"I love you. I fell in love with you that night on the beach. The baby is an added bonus, a precious gift. If there weren't a baby, I'd still want to marry you because I truly love you."

"Now. Now you love me, Carl loved me, but it was temporary. My mother said she loved me whenever she happened to come to the boarding school to visit me. 'I love you, Alida,' she'd say. 'We'll have a wonderful time, just the two of us, on your birthday,' or maybe Christmas, or spring vacation, or whenever. But it never happened because by then she'd be off with her latest man. I'd get a quick phone call from her saying that next time she'd make it up to me. I don't even know where she is at the moment, or whom she's with."

"That's all in the past, Alida."

"No, it isn't. I believe that *you* believe that you love me, Paul-Anthony. But it's only for now, for a little while. Love is like that for me, and I've accepted it. I'm not meant to have a forever love. That's just the way things are."

"No!"

"With the baby," she went on, a sob catching in her throat, "it was going to be different. A baby would return my love unconditionally. It would be a different kind of love far removed from the hurtful love I've tried to hold on to in the past. I do want this baby, Paul-Anthony, but—but it's mine. Mine."

He lunged to his feet and paced the room, back and forth, with heavy strides. He dragged a restless hand through his hair, then stopped in front of her.

"I don't know how to get through to you," he said wearily. "I'm trying so damn hard to be patient, to give you time, to understand you. But you keep throwing things at me that hurt, really hurt, Alida. You weren't going to tell me about my own child. You think I'm going to shut off my love for you like a faucet. You're slam-dunking me at every turn."

"Then leave me alone!" she exclaimed, pounding the sofa cushion with one fist. "I'm not asking anything of you, Paul-Anthony. Oh, please, just go away and let me live my life with my baby the way I planned it."

Fresh tears spilled onto her cheeks. He had to go before she weakened, she thought, before the voices of her heart spoke louder than those of her logical mind. Before she fell in love with him. Before she clung to the fragile thread of hope that maybe this time . . .

"Please, please, please, Paul-Anthony."

He drew a breath so deep, so sharp, it seemed to tear at his very soul with nearly unbearable pain. He was standing inches away from the only woman he'd ever loved, and nestled within her was their child. Inches away, he thought, but it might as well be miles, an entire universe. Gazing helplessly at her, he was filled with the greatest sense of despair and loneliness he'd ever known.

"Go," she whispered. "Please."

"I can't do that," he said, striving for control of his emotions. "I'll leave now and let you get some sleep, but I'm not disappearing from your life. You're forcing me to take steps I don't want to take, Alida. If I have to, I'll go to court to gain joint custody of our child."

She shook her head numbly. "No."

"Think about it, because I mean every word I'm saying. Every word, including my declarations of love for you. If you never come to believe in my love, then you'll give me no choice but to have at least a role in my child's life. That's not the way I want it to be. You, your love, are first and foremost in my mind and heart. If I can't have your love, then I'm sure as hell not giving up my baby too. Think about it, Alida."

He crossed the room and picked up his suit coat, then left the apartment, closing the door with more force than was necessary.

"No," she said to the silence. "Oh, no."

And then she wept until she had no more tears to shed.

"That's expensive Scotch you're tossing back, Paul-Anthony," John-Trevor said. "Not that I blame you, I guess. After what you told me about Alida, I'd say you have every right to get rip-roaring drunk. At least you're here in my apartment so when you pass out cold, you'll have a comfortable bed to nurse your hangover in."

"Right," Paul-Anthony said, and drained his glass. He refilled it immediately, then stared moodily into the amber liquid. "This isn't going to solve a thing."

"True," John-Trevor said, "but it'll numb your brain for a few hours. The lady has really laid a heavy trip on you, big brother. I've never seen you like this. You're hurtin', Paul-Anthony, and it hurts me to see it. Women. What a hundred pounds of fluff can do to a man is criminal."

"I love her," Paul-Anthony said, his speech slightly slurred. "I love Alida, my beautiful Alida. And I already love that baby because it exists, it's mine. . . . No, it's ours. Alida's and mine and . . . Ah, hell." He drained half his glass. "I love her."

"Which," John-Trevor said, "doesn't sound like the brightest thing you've ever done. This love stuff is never going to happen to me, that's for damn sure." He paused. "Before you're completely blitzed, talk to me. Are you really going to go after joint custody of the baby?"

"If I have to, but there are a lot of months between now and when that baby is born." He hiccuped. " 'Scuse me." He sank onto the sofa next to John-Trevor. "I think . . . I'd better stay sitting down."

"Good idea. So, okay, the baby is due around the first of the year. Happy New Year, one and all. And, yes, there's a lot of time between now and then. To do what?"

Paul-Anthony turned his head to look at John-Trevor, then blinked, trying to bring his brother into focus.

"To convince Alida that I'll love her forever, 'course," he said. "Yep, that's what I'm gonna do." He began to tilt precariously to one side. "Some . . . how." He landed with a thud on the leather sofa.

John-Trevor shook his head, then stood up. He leveled Paul-Anthony over one shoulder as though his brother weighed hardly more than a sack of potatoes. Snorting with disgust, he started down the hall, toward the bedrooms of the large, expensively furnished apartment.

"Women," he muttered. "Lord knows I like 'em, but it will be a cold day in hell before I ever fall in love with one. Not a chance."

Five

During the next several days, Alida could feel her nerves coiling tighter and tighter, until she envisioned herself as a human-sized spring that would go "boing" at the slightest provocation.

The scene in her apartment with Paul-Anthony, when he told her that he knew about her baby, his baby—dear heaven, *their* baby—replayed constantly in her mind. Ever present, too, was the memory of him adamantly stating he would declare his love for her *every day*, without fail.

At work she tensed whenever the telephone rang, or Lisa came into her office unexpectedly. She stiffened each night as she got out of the elevator in her apartment building.

During the seemingly endless evenings, she found herself straining to hear any sound of someone approaching her door.

But from Paul-Anthony Payton, there was total silence.

That was great, she told herself repeatedly. He'd gotten the message and had faded into the sunset.

But where was he? she'd wonder in the next instant. What was he thinking? Doing? Had the hurt she'd seen in his gorgeous eyes that night in her apartment dimmed, then disappeared? Was she out of sight and out of mind to him? Had he dismissed her as well as the baby she carried within her?

Yes, yes, her mind would say, that was what she wanted. But the voices of her heart would speak as well, taunting her with her aloneness as she lay in bed throughout the dark nights.

One week after she'd last seen Paul-Anthony, Alida arrived at the hotel fully aware that he was scheduled to meet with her that morning at ten. Lisa greeted her with a smile, but Alida was sadly aware that there was still a slight strain between them.

"My goodness," she said brightly, "you look spiffy today, Lisa." Her gaze slid over Lisa's royal blue dress, which outlined the secretary's lush figure to perfection. "That's a new dress, isn't it?"

Lisa nodded. "Paul-Anthony Payton is due here this morning. I decided to use a bit of femme fatale on that hunk. This dress ought to catch his attention. I've done my homework on the scrumptious Mr. Payton. He's seen at all sorts of cultural and charity events with a different woman on his arm every time. Beyond that, word has it, he's dedicated to his work. The man is due and overdue for a special woman in his life, and I intend to give him a run for his money."

"Lisa . . ." Alida started, then stopped. What on earth would she say? "Go for it, Lisa." Or, "Don't you dare bat your false eyelashes at that man, Lisa, because he's mine, and I'm carrying his baby"? She was losing her mind, totally. Her poor baby was going to have a cuckoo for a mother.

"You look stunning," she said, and hurried into her office.

But it was a fuming Lisa who strode into Alida's office at ten o'clock.

"That creep," she said. "Paul-Anthony Payton didn't come. He sent a tweaky twit with the message that Paul-Anthony is out of town, and you're to go over the details with this nerd."

"I see," Alida said quietly. "Well, show him in, please."

Why did she feel like crying? she asked herself. Why did the emotion sweeping through her surpass disappointment and land solidly on hurt? Why, oh, why, did she feel so incredibly lonely?

The days and nights passed . . . slowly.

Alida returned to Dr. Allen's office a month after her initial appointment, and the doctor prescribed vitamins to take daily. Her pregnancy was progressing nicely, Dr. Allen said, but Alida was slightly underweight.

"Underweight?" Alida repeated. "I'm getting very fat very fast. I can't fit into most of my clothes, and have resorted to flouncy overblouses to hide my half-open zippers."

Dr. Allen smiled. "Babies take up room, Alida. However, I'm treating you, the entire woman, not just the child. The baby is fine, you're too thin. I want you to eat more."

"Oh, mercy," Alida said, rolling her eyes.

And from Paul-Anthony Payton, continued silence.

Time ticked by . . . slowly.

In the middle of one afternoon, six weeks after Alida had last seen Paul-Anthony, Max Brewer strode into her office unannounced.

"Alida," he said, "I've just spoken to Paul-Anthony Payton on the phone."

Alida stiffened. "Oh?"

"His conference is this weekend, you know."

"I'm aware of that, Max. I've been working very closely with a member of Mr. Payton's staff. Everything is ready. I don't anticipate any problems."

"I should hope not. This conference is important to the hotel. Mr. Payton has requested that you be his escort for the final banquet Sunday night. He feels it would be a nice touch to introduce you and give you credit for handling the setup of the conference. You'd be representing the Swan, of course."

"No," Alida said, feeling the blood drain from her face. "It's out of the question. Our conferences don't include an escort for the evening."

"Alida, perhaps you didn't hear me correctly. This is a direct request from Paul-Anthony Payton."

"Have Lisa go with him. She'd be delighted."

"He specifically said he wanted to take you. He'll pick you up at eight o'clock."

"No," she said, shaking her head.

Max glared fiercely at her. "I'm not asking you to go, I'm *ordering* you to go. You seem to be forgetting that you hold this position because I was under pressure to have a woman executive at this hotel. I would have preferred to give the promotion to Jerry Nash. One slip-up, just one, and you're gone, Alida Hunter. No one can yell foul if you don't perform your job competently. You'll attend that banquet with Paul-Anthony Payton. Understood?"

"I—"

"Fine." He turned and started toward the door, then stopped. "By the way, you're putting on a lot of weight. You have an image to maintain. I'd suggest you start passing up desserts."

By the time Alida had jumped to her feet in angry protest, Max was gone, leaving her to scowl at an empty room. She sank back into her chair, her heart beating hard.

She had no choice but to go to the banquet with Paul-Anthony. She had a child to think of now, and couldn't run the risk of losing her job. If Max fired her, no one would hire her at this stage of her pregnancy.

"Damn," she said, smacking the top of her desk with her hands. "Ow. Oh, ow."

"Go back to damn," Jerry said, strolling into the office. "Take a look at this."

"What is it?" she asked, suddenly very weary. "From the expression on you face, it isn't good news."

"It sure as hell isn't. A messenger from the printer just arrived with this sample of the awards banquet program for the writers' conference." He tossed it onto Alida's desk. "Check it out."

"It's pale blue. Jerry . . ."

"I know, I know, it's supposed to be pale pink to go with their theme of pink and burgundy. Plus, it's done in block lettering instead of script. I talked to the printer and he swears that the order came from here exactly like that. He was just waiting for an okay so he could do the print run. Alida, I didn't send in an order for blue paper and block lettering."

She sighed. "All right. Did you set him straight?"

"You bet I did, but there will be a delay now. He'll redo the sample and get it here. I'll call the coordinator for the writers' conference and tell her we'll have a sample as soon as possible, but not as quickly as we'd promised."

"That's the best we can do. How did something like this happen?"

Jerry shrugged. "Damned if I know." He snatched up the blue paper and strode toward the door. "Hell."

"No joke," Alida muttered, massaging her aching temples.

And to frost the crummy cake, she thought, what on earth was she going to wear to the banquet with Paul-Anthony? None of her dresses would camouflage the cantaloupe-size lump that used to be her flat stomach. Paul-Anthony knew about the baby, but she definitely wasn't ready to announce it to the world.

And, her mind rushed on, what was Paul-Anthony up to? There had been only silence, day after day, night after night, and now there he was again, demanding that she attend the banquet with him. A banquet, she knew, that had been planned to include small intimate tables, candlelight, and a band that would play dreamy music for dancing.

She didn't want to go.

Yes, she did, her heart whispered. She'd missed Paul-Anthony so very, very much. He'd been in her thoughts almost continually, but that wasn't enough. She wanted to drink in the sight of him, hear his voice and laughter, gaze into the mesmerizing depths of his incredible blue eyes.

She'd buy a new dress that would make her feel beautiful and feminine. She'd spend hours with him, perhaps even be held in his arms as they floated across the dance floor. Like Cinderella, she'd cherish the time spent at the ball, and carefully tuck away the memories.

It would be a special night, a wondrous night. A night stolen from reality and spent with the man she loved.

"What?" Alida said, straightening abruptly.

This couldn't be true, but it was too late. She was deeply, irrevocably in love with Paul-Anthony.

Alida sank back in her chair with a funny little sound that was part giggle, part sob. She'd really done it now, she thought dismally. She'd fallen in love, broken the vow she'd made to herself never to do that again.

And again she'd chosen the wrong person to give her heart to.

Paul-Anthony, for all his great declarations of love, had walked out of her apartment, and her life, weeks before. Why he was suddenly demanding she attend the banquet with him, she didn't know. The fact remained he'd been too busy to see or talk to her since that night. His love for her was temporary.

Alida shook her head, realizing that she would burst into tears if she dwelled on her dilemma for one second longer, and reached for a file on the corner of her desk.

Work, she told herself. Do *not* think. Just work.

On Saturday Alida shopped for a dress for the banquet. In spite of her gloomy mood, she found herself smiling at her reflection in the fitting room of a small boutique.

"That's it," she said, turning back and forth in front of the triple mirror. "It's perfect."

The strapless dress was the color of a sunkissed peach, with a snug-fitting bodice that emphasized her swelling breasts. The full, calf-length skirt, gathered at the waist, adequately concealed her burgeoning belly.

It was sophisticated and classy, she decided, and certainly more attractive than the business suits and blue jeans Paul-Anthony had seen her in previously. She'd buy evening sandals, a new clutch bag, and away she'd go, looking utterly smashing.

When she entered the lobby of her apartment building, the security guard jumped to his feet.

"Miss Hunter," he said, "there was a delivery for you."

"Oh? Well, fine. I'll take it."

"Well . . . um, it was a bit more than you could carry. I contacted the manager, and he said I should let the delivery people into your apartment with the passkey. I watched them every second, so don't worry about that. I wanted to tell you so you wouldn't be . . . um, surprised when you went upstairs."

"I see," Alida said, thoroughly puzzled. "Thank you."

When she stepped into her apartment, her eyes widened and her mouth dropped open. Brightly colored helium balloons bounced against the ceiling of the living room, nearly hiding it completely. A long string was attached to each balloon, and at the bottom of the string was a small white envelope.

She stepped cautiously into the room and set her packages on the sofa, then opened one of the envelopes.

I love you, Alida, the message on the card read.

She opened another envelope, then another

and another. All of them contained a card with the same words. *I love you, Alida.*

Paul-Anthony, she realized, had sent a balloon for each day they'd been apart, declaring his love for her just as he'd vowed he would.

She stared up at her rainbow-colored ceiling, her mind racing. Why? she wondered. Why had he done this? After all those silent weeks, when she'd convinced herself he had put her out of his mind, and most definitely evicted her from his heart, he did this. Why?

The baby? No, that didn't make sense. She knew and Paul-Anthony knew that he had the money and power to take her to court and gain joint custody of their child. That was a given.

So why the silence, and then these balloons and the messages of love? Why the silence, and then the demand that she attend the banquet with him? Why the silence, which had proven yet again that love was not meant for her, and then . . . ? Oh, she was so confused, muddled, and thoroughly exhausted.

Pushing the dangling envelopes out of her path, she went into the bedroom, where she curled up on the bed to take a long, dreamless nap.

During the hours left to her before the banquet on Sunday, Alida took herself in hand

and delivered a deluge of firm lectures regarding her conduct while with Paul-Anthony Payton.

She would *not,* she vowed, fall prey to the Cinderella syndrome, believing a glitzy, glamorous evening spent with a handsome prince, aka Paul-Anthony Payton, would last beyond midnight.

She would *not* succumb to the romantic atmosphere created at the hotel, nor to the sensual magnetism of her escort.

She could *not* grant herself one unguarded moment of love, because to do so would be very, very dangerous.

She was furious enough at herself for falling in love with Paul-Anthony. She would, at least, salvage her tattered self-esteem by not giving him one clue as to her true feelings for him.

"I am in control," she said aloud Sunday afternoon, pointing one finger in the air. It struck one of the envelopes hanging from a balloon. The balloon shifted, bumping the one close to it, shoving it into the next, then the next. . . . Her entire rainbow-colored ceiling squeaked and moved, and white envelopes danced a jig.

"Oh, for Pete's sake."

Sunday evening, Alida applied her makeup with special care, brushed her strawberry-blond curls until they shone, dabbed on flowery cologne, then slipped into her classy, feminine dress.

Her pearls were around her neck, her gleaming new shoes were on her feet, her clutch bag was in her hand, and her stomach was paying hostess to a zillion butterflies.

"I'm fine," she said as she left the bedroom. A knock sounded at the door. "No, I'm not."

She knew it was Paul-Anthony having done whatever he did to get past the security guard without being announced. It was Paul-Anthony, the man she loved, the father of her baby. So? No big deal. Oh, Lord, she was a wreck.

She took a steadying breath, mentally rushed through one of her lectures, and lifted her chin. Brushing aside the envelopes, she crossed the room and opened the door.

"Hello, Alida," Paul-Anthony said.

How dare he? she fumed. Oh, the despicableness—was that a word?—of the man. How dare he stand there in a custom-tailored tuxedo, complete with a sparkling white shirt with tiny pleats, looking as though he'd just escaped from a fashion magazine? How dare he wear a musky aftershave that assaulted her senses? How dare he have shoulders that wide, legs that long, hips that narrow, hair that thick, and such an incredibly handsome face? He was just so—so rude.

"Good evening, Paul-Anthony," she said coolly. "Please, come in."

He stepped into the apartment and a grin spread across his face as he saw the balloons.

"Ah, they arrived," he said.

"It was a tad much, don't you think?" Good grief, she sounded witchy, but it was her only defense. *She had to stay in control.* "Balloons are nice, but this is ridiculous."

"No, it isn't," he said, still smiling as he met her gaze. "It's one balloon with one declaration of love for every day we were apart. As for today . . . I love you, Alida. That dress is sensational."

"Thank you. For the compliment about my dress," she tacked on quickly. She lifted her chin a fraction higher. "Paul-Anthony, I don't know why you disappeared off the face of the earth, then— "

"You noticed I wasn't around? Terrific."

"*Then,*" she went on, glaring at him, "did your balloon routine, *then* insisted that I attend this banquet with you. I don't know why, nor do I care. I'm going with you tonight because my boss demanded that I do so."

"I left you alone to give you time to think, sort things through. I wanted you with me tonight because I've missed you more than I can say."

"Oh." She ruthlessly squelched the warm

flutter of pleasure deep within her. "You needn't have explained because I just said that I didn't care."

"Oh, that's right, I forgot." He paused. "How's our baby?"

"The child in question is fine. I'm fat, the baby is growing at the proper rate. Furthermore, I have come to realize that as the father, you do have certain minuscule rights. I'm sure we can work out an acceptable visitation schedule when the time comes. Shall we go?"

Paul-Anthony narrowed his eyes. "Since we've been apart, did you take a course in how to be a snooty shrew?"

"That, sir," Alida said with a toss of her head, "was uncalled for. It's time to leave, Mr. Payton, or you're going to be late for your own banquet."

She swept out the door with what she decided was a wonderfully dramatic flair. Paul-Anthony chuckled softly, then followed her, giving the balloons a two-fingered salute before he closed the door.

The moment Alida entered the ballroom at the hotel, she had one depressing thought: The person who had organized the event should be shot. Said person being Miss Alida Hunter.

The room was romance waiting to happen. The crystal chandeliers were dimmed to a faint shimmer, accentuating the candlelight that glowed from hurricane lamps in the center of each small table.

The gleaming dance floor at the end of the room held the promise of things to come. Dancing in the arms of a special man, swaying to dreamy music as though there were no one else in the room but the two of them.

The other guests were resplendent; men in tuxedos, women in exquisite dresses, and each woman wore the delicate orchid corsage she and Paul-Anthony had decided upon.

It was all so lovely, Alida mused, and Paul-Anthony was by far the most handsome, most magnificent man there. She felt pure feminine smugness as she noticed the appreciative glances he received from other women. But Alida Hunter was on Paul-Anthony's arm. *She* was his lady. And little did they know that he was *her* man.

Stop it, Alida, she admonished herself. Control was the key word. She had to retain control of herself, of her emotions. There must be no clue, no hint whatsoever, that she was deeply in love with Paul-Anthony.

He led her across the room, one hand resting lightly at the back of her waist. He nodded and smiled at all who greeted him, but didn't stop to chat or to introduce Alida to anyone.

Their table was right by the dance floor, but set in the shadows, its candle flickering in welcome. He picked up an orchid corsage from the table.

"For you," he said.

"Oh, well, thank you," she said. "I didn't expect . . . Thank you."

He pinned the corsage to her dress with the expertise, she noted, of a man who had performed the task many times before. Good point, she told herself. She'd do well to remember that Paul-Anthony was known, according to Lisa, to have a different woman on his arm at each of the various functions he attended. He was a here-today-gone-tomorrow playboy. That knowledge would aid her control campaign immensely.

She smiled her thanks as he assisted her with her chair, then froze when he sat opposite her.

Oh, darn, she thought. What the candlelight did for Paul-Anthony's attractive, tanned face was not fair. And his hair gleamed like ebony, the silver strands at his temples shining like starlight.

Her heart pounded so hard, it nearly hurt, and she suddenly had trouble breathing. She could see the desire in his eyes, and tore her gaze from his.

"I have to make a brief announcement," he said, "thanking everyone for coming, and wishing them a safe journey home. I'll introduce you as the person responsible for this top-notch conference."

"That really isn't necessary," she said, still not looking at him.

"Yes, is it. This conference went as smoothly as glass, and it's due to your attention to detail. I could tell you some real horror stories of past conferences my company has had. I highly respect the work you do, Alida, and you deserve the recognition."

"Thank you," she mumbled.

"I'll be back in a few minutes," he said, "then the rest of the evening is ours to enjoy."

He left, and Alida was finally able to draw in a deep breath. She searched her mind for one of her many lectures to herself, but found none. Her entire sight was filled with images of Paul-Anthony.

She heard him speaking into a microphone, and thankfully recognized her name when he introduced her. She stood on cue and managed to smile. Paul-Anthony told everyone to have fun, then with a wave to acknowledge the thundering applause, returned to the table.

"Done," he said, sitting back down. "Ah, good. Waiters are practically swarming into the room with the dinners. I'm starving."

And she was dying, Alida thought. She wasn't going to survive this. Yes, yes, she would. Control, Alida. Get it together.

"Your drinks," a waiter said, appearing beside her chair. He consulted a paper on his tray. "Scotch on the rocks for you, sir, and for the lady, ginger ale with a cherry."

As the waiter set their drinks down, Alida stared at Paul-Anthony. He smiled back.

"I wouldn't want you to get a case of the hiccups," he said as the waiter walked away.

She scowled at him. "Paul-Anthony, go to the dentist."

He laughed, then his expression became serious. "You claim that you've put that night in the mist out of your mind," he said, "yet you remember what we talked about. What else do you remember about that night? What memories have you stored away?"

"Paul-Anthony, don't," she said softly. "Please don't."

He started to speak, then shook his head. "All right," he said, sounding weary. "Here's our dinner. We'll concentrate on prime rib and baked potatoes."

It was a good thing, Alida thought, as they ate in silence, that Paul-Anthony had told her the hunk of meat was prime rib and that blob was a baked potato, because it all tasted like sawdust.

She wanted—oh, what an absurd picture it

created in her mind—but she wanted to sweep the dishes off the table, leap onto the linen tablecloth, then land smack-dab in Paul-Anthony's lap. She'd wrap her arms around his neck, kiss him until he couldn't breathe, then tell him four-hundred and twenty-two times that she loved him.

Then, Alida mused on dreamily, after she'd agreed to marry him as soon as possible, they'd discuss names for the baby, where they would live, and on and on.

No, she'd tell him. She didn't need an engagement ring, but thank you for the thought, sweetheart. A plain gold wedding band would be fine, and she'd be very pleased if he'd wear one too. He would? Oh, that was divine, just simply divine.

"Alida?" Paul-Anthony said.

She gasped. "What? Oh, hello. I mean . . . yes?"

"Are you all right? You have the strangest expression on your face, and you've been holding your fork in midair for several minutes."

She blinked, stared at the fork, then popped the speared piece of meat into her mouth. She chewed, swallowed, and managed a small smile.

"I'm perfectly perfect," she said. Except for being totally insane, she added to herself. Such ridiculous daydreams. The only saving grace was that Paul-Anthony wasn't capable of peering into her scrambled brain. "This is a delicious dinner. Utterly . . . divine."

"Yes, it's very good," he said, frowning at her. "Would you care for some more ginger ale?"

"Oh, no, no, one drink is my limit." She shrugged. "Little joke there." She cleared her throat. "Yes . . . well . . . would you excuse me for a moment, Paul-Anthony? I'd like to go to the powder room."

"Of course." He stood and assisted her with her chair.

"Thank you," she said, and hurried away.

Paul-Anthony sat back down and stared at his plate. He hadn't tasted one bite, he realized, and he certainly didn't want any more to eat. Dammit, he was making no progress in his attempt to convince Alida that he would love her for all time, that they belonged together forever.

He leaned back, crossing his arms over his chest, and squinted into the candlelight.

Alida wasn't totally impervious to him, he decided. She remembered every detail of their night in the fog, of that he was certain. The fact that she was acting strangely indicated that she was rattled, definitely affected by being with him.

All those were points in his favor, he reasoned, but they weren't enough. Staying away from her, giving her time to think, had accomplished nothing more than giving *him* long, sleepless nights. Declaring his love for her every day with spoken words, flowers, and balloons hadn't made her swoon in delight.

So, he asked himself. Now what? He'd have to regroup *again,* start over *again.* And he would. Because what she didn't seem to realize was that he intended to win.

Alida Hunter was his.

And he loved her more with every beat of his slightly battered heart.

Six

When Alida returned to the table, Paul-Anthony smiled at her pleasantly. He nodded at the waiter, who cleared their plates away, then voiced his approval as strawberry shortcake with a crown of whipped cream was set in front of them.

"Don't you like strawberry shortcake?" he asked as Alida frowned at the dessert.

"Oh, yes, I do," she said, looking up at him. "I was just thinking about a remark my boss, Max Brewer, made. He told me I was gaining weight and should start passing up desserts."

"In the first place," Paul-Anthony said, keeping his voice even with great effort, "Brewer has no right to say anything about how much you weigh. It has nothing to do with the manner in which you perform your duties."

"*I* know that, but Max is from the old school."

"In the second place," Paul-Anthony went on, his jaw tightening, "you and I both know that you're gaining weight because of the baby. That's none of Brewer's business."

"From a legal standpoint," Alida said, "you're right, but . . ." She glanced around.

"No one can hear what we're saying," Paul-Anthony said. "With the way the tables are arranged, plus the good acoustics in here, voices don't carry. I haven't heard one word of anyone else's conversations. It's just a low hum. Alida, talk to me. What's with Brewer?"

"He promoted me under duress, so to speak. The head office ordered him to place a woman in an executive position. He would have preferred to give Jerry Nash, my assistant, the spot of director when it came open. I knew at the time that I'd won by default, but I was determined to do an excellent job. And I have."

"Go on," Paul-Anthony said.

"Max is still angry over being told what to do. He considers this hotel his, and actually seems to forget at times that it's part of a chain that has a board of directors. Max is waiting for me to make a major mistake so that he can fire me. When he finds out I'm pregnant, he'll be furious. I know how his mind works, and he'll hate the idea of an unwed mother having an important position in *his* hotel."

"Tough. If he fires you because of the baby, you can sue the pants off him."

"Oh, he wouldn't be that foolish. No, he would wait and watch for the slightest slip-up, then base his case on incompetence. I've been aware of his attitude since I got the promotion, and I've learned to live with it. It's just that now I have to keep this job so I can take proper care of the baby."

Dammit, Paul-Anthony thought, Alida wouldn't have to worry about Brewer if she'd only marry him. She could take off as much time as she wanted for the baby, and get another job later if she chose to.

Easy, Payton, he told himself. He had to keep his mouth shut. He had just figured out his new plan of action.

"I apologize, Paul-Anthony," she said, bringing him from his thoughts. "I shouldn't have dumped all this on you. It's only that . . . Well, you're a very good listener." She smiled. "And I'm about to eat this dessert down to the last crumb."

"Go for it," he said, matching her smile.

She took a bite and closed her eyes for a moment. "Mmm. Delicious." She looked at him again. "Your friend, Dr. Nelson, said that the Payton boys were roughnecks. Tell me more about your brothers. Are you close?"

"Very close. John-Trevor lives here and . . ."

Alida listened intently as Paul-Anthony told her amusing stories of the young Paytons' escapades. She found herself relaxing, her laughter natural as she polished off her strawberry shortcake.

Oh, this was nice, she mused. She and Paul-Anthony were chatting easily, enjoying each other's company. She should not, she supposed, have told him about Max, but now, somehow, the problem wasn't weighing so heavily on her.

This, she realized, was one of the rewards she would reap if she were part of a couple, half of a whole. Someone would be there to listen to all the major and minor victories and defeats of her life, the exciting and the mundane. This was being in love.

Was it possible that Paul-Anthony's love for her would last forever? Would his daily declarations of love stretch into infinity, for as long as they both lived? Should she dare to hope . . .

No! her mind shouted. Her vows of self-control were being swept away by the proximity of Paul-Anthony, by the romantic atmosphere of the ballroom, and by the urgings of her heart. She mustn't allow that to happen, for to love was to lose.

"The band is setting up," Paul-Anthony said. "I imagine everyone is looking forward to dancing."

She certainly was, Alida thought. She was anticipating being held in Paul-Anthony's strong arms while they swayed to the music, danced until dawn. But, no, it was far too dangerous. She was too vulnerable, and her control was slipping from her grasp.

"Paul-Anthony," she said quickly. "I'm—I'm really very tired. It's been a lovely evening, but I think it would be best if I went home. I realize that this is your conference, and you certainly can't get up and leave, so I'll take a taxi. Yes, that's the best plan. I'll just pop myself into a cab and be safely home in a jiffy."

That's it! Paul-Anthony thought. Alida Hunter was absolutely, positively falling in love with him. She was broadcasting it like a neon sign. He'd bet his last dollar that the thought of them dancing together had created for her the same sensual pictures that were flitting through his mind. And she was running like a frightened little kitten because she loved him and she was afraid to love. Patience, Payton, patience.

"I should have realized you were tired, Alida," he said calmly. "I mean, after all, mothers-to-be are supposed to get plenty of rest. This conference is officially over, so I'll take you home. No problem." He got to his feet. "Ready?"

Didn't he want to argue the point a bit? Alida wondered. It wasn't *that* late, and since it was Sunday she hadn't put in a day's work at the hotel, and . . . Oh, be quiet and go home, she told herself.

As they drove to Alida's apartment building, Paul-Anthony tuned the radio to a station playing peppy music. He hummed along and tapped his fingers on the steering wheel.

Alida kept glancing over at him, acutely aware that her rosy glow and dreamy state of mind were deteriorating rapidly.

She should count her lucky stars that she would soon be safely home and no longer with Paul-Anthony. But, darn it, did he have to be downright cheerful about ending their evening together so early, so abruptly? The least the man could do was sulk, or be a tad crabby. And it really was sad that she was providing such a cuckoo mother for her baby.

When they entered her apartment, Paul-Anthony planted his hands on his hips and stared up at the multicolored balloons decorating the ceiling.

"You're right," he said, shifting his gaze to her. "That's rather ridiculous. It wrecks your decor, and the balloons will slowly start to come down as the helium seeps out. They'll be a terrible nuisance."

"Oh, well, they're very pretty. It's like having my own rainbow and—"

"No, no, you don't have to be polite about it. It was a dumb thing to do." He ran one hand over his chin. "Compromise is called for here. On the days that I actually see you, I'll tell you that I love you. On the other days, I won't pull some corny stunt like roses or balloons to let you know."

"But—"

"Fair enough? Good. Well, I'm off so you can get your rest." He brushed his lips over hers. "Thank you for a terrific evening. Good night, Alida."

"But—"

"Sleep well." He closed the door quietly behind him, leaving Alida blinking in bemusement.

"But—" she said again, then threw up her hands. "Alida, go to bed."

"So, do you get it, John-Trevor?" Paul-Anthony asked his brother. "This is a brilliant plan. You could learn a thing or two from your big brother."

"About women?" John-Trevor said. "No thanks, Paul-Anthony. I enjoy them, but I have no desire even to *begin* to understand them." He frowned and shook his head. "Women are so emotional, so complicated.

Are you positive this idea of yours is going to work?"

Paul-Anthony got up from the sofa and began to pace John-Trevor's living room. "I've struck out at the plate with everything else I've tried," he said. "Alida *is* in love with me, John-Trevor, I know she is. The signs are all there, but she's still hiding behind those protective walls of hers. I'm chipping away at them, but the going is slow. So, a new plan."

"Sneaky plan," John-Trevor said, chuckling.

"Whatever. I'm getting desperate." Paul-Anthony stopped pacing and looked at his brother. "I stayed away from Alida, and it served its purpose in that she missed me. That's not good enough."

"So now you're going to stick like glue."

"Yes, but—and here's where I prove what a genius I am—I'll be on the scene as a concerned father-to-be. Oh, I'll tell her that I love her each time I see her, because that's something I need to do. But it will be rather casual, laid-back."

"As in, 'Oh, by the way, I love you'?"

"Something like that."

"Sounds dangerous to me, Paul-Anthony."

"No, no, it's great. She'll think I've shifted my focus to the baby and that she's an afterthought. She'll relax, let down her guard. How can I be a threat when my thoughts are centered on the baby? I'll be there, but as a

father, not as a man. There's nothing frightening about fathers. They're nice people. But
while she thinks we're operating on a totally
father-mother plane, I'll be getting close to
Alida Hunter, the woman, without her being
aware that it's happening. This is terrific."

"And dangerous," John-Trevor said. "Do you
want a drink?"

"No, thanks."

"Well, *I* need one. *You're* the one in love,
and *my* nerves are shot. I wish you'd hurry up
and just marry Alida."

"I will," Paul-Anthony said smugly. "You
can count on it."

"Right," John-Trevor said dryly, and poured
himself a hefty drink.

Late Monday afternoon Alida finished double-
checking a list of details for a small gathering
of automotive dealers who were having a
luncheon-with-speaker at the hotel. She ro-
tated her neck back and forth in an attempt
to loosen the tightened muscles, then stood
and walked over to her office window.

She hadn't slept well the night before. She'd
gone to bed immediately after Paul-Anthony's
hasty exit, but had tossed and turned, unable to quiet the confusion in her mind.

Alida sighed and placed her hands lightly
on her stomach. Did the tiny entity within

her know she'd had a restless night? she wondered. Soon she'd begin to feel the baby move. Was it a delicate little girl, or a sturdy little boy? Would it have her coloring, or Paul-Anthony's? She should start making a list of possible names for the baby and—

"Oh, my God. You're pregnant!"

Alida spun around in surprise. Lisa was standing by the desk, gaping at her.

"The way you were half turned from the window," Lisa went on, "and how you had your hands placed, I could clearly see that you're— Oh, Alida, why didn't you tell me?" She shook her head. "I can't believe this. I thought, I really thought we were such close friends. I've told you my innermost secrets and . . . First the roses and your refusal to divulge who sent them and now . . ." Tears filled her eyes. "I guess I assumed too much about our friendship."

Alida hurried across the room and gave Lisa a quick hug. "Don't say that. We *are* friends, good ones, and I cherish our friendship. Everything has happened so quickly that I've been trying to sort things through in my mind. I should have come to you, shared my troubles, because heaven knows I could have used a shoulder to cry on more than once. Lisa, please don't be hurt or angry. My life has been turned upside down, and I wouldn't want to destroy our friendship on top of everything else."

"I'm being too sensitive," Lisa said, sniffling. "That's one of my major flaws, and I try to cover it up with a brassy facade. My hurt feelings are mine to deal with, Alida, and I'll do the best I can. The real issue at the moment is you. Lord, a baby. Is it Carl Ambrey's?"

"Carl? No. Good grief, no."

"Well, praise be for that much. Who's the father?"

Alida crossed the room to close the door, then turned to face Lisa again.

"Lisa, do I have your word that you won't tell anyone that I'm pregnant?"

"Yes, of course, but you can't hide it for long."

"I know. Max is going to fly into a rage. I have to prove to him that I can function as efficiently as I always have, so he'll have no grounds to fire me. He wouldn't dare dismiss me on the basis that I'm an unwed mother."

"True, but why don't you marry the father? Does he know about the baby?"

"Yes, he knows, but I don't want to get married. I had no intention of falling in love with him, either, but . . . At least he doesn't know how I feel about him."

"Alida, you're allowing your past to dictate your future. You have a child to think of."

"I *am* concentrating on my child. I'll be a

good mother, a wonderful mother. It will be just the two of us, the baby and me. That's better than having the man, the father, up and leave when he's tired of us. That's how love is for me. Temporary."

"Oh, Alida, that isn't etched in stone."

"Lisa, there are just some people who aren't meant to love and be loved. Why things are set up that way in this crazy world, I don't know. What I do know is that I'm one of those people."

Lisa sighed and shook her head. "Well, we'll put that part on hold for now. But, Alida, are you going to tell me who the father is?"

Alida took a steadying breath, then lifted her chin. She met Lisa's questioning gaze directly.

"Yes, I'll tell you," she said, her voice trembling slightly. "It's—it's Paul-Anthony Payton."

The color drained from Lisa's face, and she took a step backward. "Paul-Anthony . . ." Her gaze dropped to Alida's stomach, then collided with her eyes once again. "But that's impossible. I mean, you just met him for the first time here, when he came to make arrangements for his conference."

"No," Alida said quietly. "I'd . . . met him a little over six weeks before that. It's very complicated, Lisa."

"No, it isn't, not really." Lisa said, her eyes brimming with tears again. "You let me make a fool of myself over him. I went on and on about how handsome he was, how he was overdue for a special woman in his life, and about me being it. I even bought a new dress, decked myself out to the nines to impress him. How you must have been laughing at silly Lisa, because there you stood the whole time pregnant with the man's baby."

"No," Alida said in anguish. "It wasn't like that."

"You consider yourself unlucky in love, Alida Hunter, and I'm realizing that I'm lousy at choosing friends."

"Lisa, please, listen to me—"

"No, I've heard enough. Oh, dear Lord, I've definitely heard enough." She ran from the room, leaving the door open behind her.

"Lisa . . ." Alida called, then sighed with defeat.

Sitting back down behind her desk, she stared at the open doorway. So many lives, she thought, were being affected by what had taken place that foggy night months before. Where would it end? How many people would be hurt, how many tears shed?

"Hey, boss," Jerry said, sauntering into her office, "what's doin'? Your secretary has escaped from the zoo, by the way. Lisa's not out there."

"She . . . isn't feeling well, Jerry. Was there something you needed?"

"The writers' conference." He slouched into one of the chairs in front of Alida's desk. "The reservations for rooms are coming in, and we have a mess on our hands like you wouldn't believe."

"What do you mean?"

"Someone screwed up. The reservation computer shows only half the number of rooms needed as being blocked off. The rest are footloose and fancy free, *and* there are John Q. Citizens booked into some of them."

Alida jumped to her feet. "That's impossible. How could that have happened? We'll have to go see the reservation manager right now and get this straightened out. Jerry, those rooms were blocked off weeks ago. How on earth . . . Why are you staring at me? What is your problem?"

He slowly stood up. "Either you've been on a hot fudge sundae binge, or the stork got the wrong address for a delivery. Holy hell, Alida, are you pregnant?"

Her cheeks flushed hotly, but she kept her shoulders straight. "Yes, I am, Jerry. I'm going to have a baby, and I'm thrilled about it."

"You're a tad short in the husband department, aren't you?"

"We're living in the nineties, not the Dark Ages. Single parents aren't uncommon."

"Oh, yeah? Tell that to Max."

"Max will have no cause for complaint, because I'll do my job as efficiently as I always have."

"Oh, man, you are in for trouble. Max is going to hit the roof and—"

"Enough, Jerry," she interrupted. "I suggest we concentrate on unraveling this mess with the rooms for the writers' conference. Come on, let's go see the reservation manager."

It was after nine o'clock before Alida let herself into her apartment and closed the door with a weary sigh.

The room reservation dilemma had been straightened out, but she was thoroughly exhausted. She still couldn't fathom how such a blatant error had been made. Those rooms had been blocked off, then suddenly the computer had showed that half of them were available for general use. It just didn't make sense, any more than the printer getting the wrong instructions for the banquet program had.

With another sigh, Alida started toward the kitchen, then saw the red light blinking on her answering machine, indicating she had a message. She pressed the playback button and waited to hear who had called.

"Alida," a deep voice said, "this is Paul-Anthony. I have to leave immediately for London to wrap up a deal over there. My secretary will know where I'm staying if you need me.

Take good care of our baby while I'm gone."
He paused. "Oh, I love you. I'll phone you
when I get back in a week or so."

She listened to the message again, then
erased it.

"If you need me," she said aloud. She *did*
need Paul-Anthony, immediately. She was so
tired she could have wept. She needed to feel
his strong, comforting arms around her, to
hear his marvelous voice telling her she wasn't
alone. She didn't want him to go to London,
because she loved him, she'd miss him, and . . .

Oh, dear Lord, she thought, where was her
mind taking her? She *was* alone, and that's
how it was going to be. Later, she'd have the
baby with her, but . . .

She looked at the answering machine again.

The baby, she mused. Paul-Anthony had
said she should take good care of their baby.
He hadn't said to take good care of herself.
And his declaration of love had seemed almost like an afterthought.

With a frown on her face, Alida went into
the kitchen to feed Scooter and herself.

The "week or so" that Paul-Anthony had
said he'd be in London slipped into two weeks,
then on to a third. Alida received packages
express mail and some by courier from England
containing gifts for the baby; a musical teddy

bear, a hand-carved wooden mobile of brightly painted soldiers, an enchanting cloth book with pictures of animals. The cards enclosed with each simply said, *Love, Paul-Anthony.*

At work Lisa was cordial but cool.

As time went by, Alida missed Paul-Anthony more and more. On the evening that marked exactly four weeks since he'd gone to London, she answered a knock at her apartment door to find him standing before her.

Paul-Anthony Payton.

Her heart quickened as she gazed at him, feeling as though she were drowning in his sky-blue eyes. She wanted to fling herself into his arms and hold him fast, savoring his strength and warmth.

"Well, the traveler returns," she said, amazed her voice was steady. "And you charmed the security guard as usual." She stepped back. "Come in, Paul-Anthony."

Oh, Lord, she was beautiful, Paul-Anthony thought as he entered the apartment. For all the time he'd been gone, the need to see her had been a constant ache. His stay in London had seemed like an eternity. He wanted to pull her close and kiss her with the pent-up love and desire of weeks, but he had to remember the plan.

"So, how have you been?" he asked. His gaze slid over her, taking in the noticeable bulge beneath her loose-fitting blue caftan—as well as the enticing tumble of her strawberry-blond hair, her sultry, tempting mouth, her— He cleared his throat. "And how's the baby?"

Alida closed the door. "We're fine, both of us. The baby is moving a lot now. I'm just starting my sixth month, and the gifts you sent were lovely. Did your business go as you anticipated?"

"No. It was a tangle of details, which is why I was gone so long." He paused. "I love you. I've gotten out of the habit of saying that because I haven't seen you."

And out of the habit of feeling it? Alida wondered. Was Paul-Anthony's love dying, fading into oblivion?

"Would you care for something to drink?" she asked.

"No, thanks. Could we sit down?"

"Of course."

She waited until he'd settled onto the sofa, then chose a straight-back chair. Their eyes met and time seemed to stop.

I love you, Paul-Anthony, Alida thought.

Oh, Alida, Paul-Anthony thought, *I love you so damn much.*

"Is everything going all right for you at work?" he asked abruptly.

"Where?" She blinked. "Oh, work. The hotel. Well, yes, sort of. What I mean is, it's very obvious that I'm pregnant, and my boss was livid when I told him. I just stood my ground and said it had nothing to do with my ability to perform my job. But Max is hovering around now like a vulture, waiting for me to make a major mistake."

"Is it good for you . . . I mean, the baby, to be under such constant stress?"

"The doctor says everything is fine."

"Well, I hope so. We can't have a stressed-out kid arriving on the scene. I've done some reading about babies, and it's fascinating. Do you play soothing music for the baby, talk to him, read him stories?"

"Read him stories? Paul-Anthony, for heaven's sake, I'm not going to sit here with a big picture book and read it to the baby."

He frowned. "Oh. Well, I could do it. You could just ignore me, and I'd read him a story."

"No."

"At least give it some thought."

"You're really getting into your role of a father, aren't you?" she asked quietly.

Go for it, Payton, he told himself. That was a perfect opening for him to lay it on thick. He mustn't tell Alida of all the sleepless nights he'd spent in London, of how he'd had John-Trevor checking on her every day to be sure she was all right, of how many times he'd fought the urge to call her just so he could hear her voice. He mustn't say that he loved her even more deeply than before.

"Oh, yes," he said. "I'm very excited about

being a father. I don't care if it's a girl or a boy, it's going to be great. I've got a lot of studying to do. You know, books on being a parent, that sort of thing, but I'll be ready when the time comes."

"That's—that's very nice," Alida said. Oh, dear heaven, it *was* happening, she thought. Paul-Anthony was shifting his emotions to the baby. Oh, not yet, Paul-Anthony, please. Couldn't he hold her one more time, kiss her, make her feel feminine and beautiful? "I'm sure you'll be a wonderful father."

Yes, he would, Paul-Anthony thought, because he wanted this baby very much. But he wanted Alida, too, as his wife. They could move into his huge house, or buy a new one if Alida preferred and—

"I'm going to paint the nursery this weekend," she said.

"Here?"

"Well, of course. This is where I live, where the baby will live."

"Right. What time do you want me to be here?"

"Pardon me?"

"On Saturday, to help paint the nursery. I'd like to be a part of getting the baby's room ready."

"Oh . . . well . . ."

"Fathers do that," he said. And husbands.

Dammit, this new plan of his was creating a knot in his gut the size of a bowling ball.

"Nine o'clock on Saturday morning," she said. "Now, if you'll excuse me, Paul-Anthony, I'm very tired. Things have been hectic at the hotel because of a series of mishaps in connection with a big writers' conference that's coming up."

"What kind of mishaps?"

She sighed. "Things that shouldn't be happening. The printer received the wrong instructions for the programs for the awards banquet, rooms weren't properly reserved, then just this week we discovered that the tote bags each conference attendee receives were sent to the Swan in San Francisco. Fortunately, the person up there called the other Swan hotels and found out that the bags belonged to us. It doesn't make sense, any of it. Yes, the errors were caught early on, but if they hadn't been . . ." She shook her head.

Frowning, Paul-Anthony leaned forward to rest his elbows on his knees, making a steeple of his fingers. He stared at the far wall for a minute. Two minutes.

"Paul-Anthony?" Alida said at last.

He straightened and gazed at her. "Did it occur to you that someone may be trying to make you look inefficient?"

Her eyes widened. "You mean, someone is deliberately causing these mistakes to happen? Sabotage? That sounds like something out of a bad movie. It's really absurd."

"Is it?" he asked quietly. "You said yourself that Max Brewer is looking for a reason to fire you."

"But Max wouldn't do anything to diminish the quality of service at the Swan. He's practically paranoid about that hotel, as though everything that happens there reflects directly on him. No, Max wouldn't attempt to sabotage something as important as this conference. It's a feather in his cap to have won the bid on it."

"The mistakes are being caught before they cause any serious problems."

"Yes, that's true but . . . No, I won't even consider the idea that someone is maliciously . . ." She paused. "Granted, there doesn't seem to be any reasonable explanation for what has happened, but still . . . Oh, good Lord, it's too sinister even to think about. Darn it, I wish you hadn't brought it up. Now I'm afraid I'll be looking for shadows lurking in the corners."

"I didn't intend to frighten you, Alida. Maybe I'm reading too much into this because of my brother, John-Trevor. He's a licensed detective, and his firm does a little of everything, from setting up security systems to cloak and dagger assignments like industrial espionage, or being bodyguards, the whole nine yards. I think John-Trevor would agree with me that with the evidence you presented, this bears watching."

"Well, *I* don't agree. Okay, Max would love to fire me, but this whole scenario you're creating is . . . is"—she swallowed heavily—"terrifying."

"Hey," Paul-Anthony said, getting to his feet, "I really have frightened you." He closed the distance between them and took her hands in his, pulling her gently to her feet. Wrapping his arms around her, he nestled her as close to him as her round stomach would allow. "I'm sorry, Alida. I shouldn't have gone on like that."

Alida leaned her head on his chest and sighed, wondering absently if the soft sound conveyed the combined sense of contentment and desire she felt when he held her.

He was so strong, and he smelled so good, and the heat emanating from his massive body warmed her right down to her toes. She loved him. Oh, dear heaven, how she loved him.

This was a mistake, Paul-Anthony thought. Desire pulsed through him, heating his blood and hardening his body. He loved this woman, and needed desperately to make love with her. He would place his hand on her naked stomach and connect with the child inside her that they'd created. He had to move Alida away from him before he did something foolish.

"Alida . . ."

She tilted her head back to look up at him. "Yes?"

"I—oh, hell," he muttered, then his mouth melted over hers.

The kiss was fire, hungry, licking flames that consumed them. Their tongues met, and their passions soared. They drank deeply of each other as their hearts raced and their breathing became labored in the quiet room. The desire within them lifted them away from reality, closer and closer to the point of no return.

Paul-Anthony tore his mouth from Alida's and stepped back, causing her to stagger slightly.

"I didn't mean for that to happen," he said, his voice rough. "It just . . . happened. I think . . ." He took a deep breath. "I think you should put the baby to bed now and get some rest. Well, I mean, you should go to bed because the baby can't go without you. Right? Right. Sleep. That's what you both need."

"Paul-Anthony, I—"

"So, I'll just get out of here and let you do that. Get some sleep." Then, not knowing what else to do, he patted Alida on the top of the head. " 'Night." He turned and nearly ran out of the apartment.

"But . . ." Alida started, then placed one hand on the top of her head. "He patted me on the head and told me to get some sleep? He actually patted me on the— Oh, what a lunatic."

She sank back onto the chair, resting one elbow on an arm and cupping her chin in her hand.

Paul-Anthony hadn't meant to kiss her, she thought. He'd seemed, in fact, extremely sorry that he'd kissed her.

His love, which she'd known all along was temporary, was definitely fading fast, disappearing like a puff of dust on a windy day. All of his thoughts and emotions were now focused on the baby.

That was fine, she told herself. It was, in actuality, the way it should be.

And she'd never been so miserable in her entire life.

Seven

As Alida walked across the hotel parking lot, she realized she had very mixed emotions about it being Friday.

A part of her, like anyone who worked, was in a TGIF mode, ready for two days off. Another section of her mind kept informing her that Saturday followed Friday, and Paul-Anthony was due at her apartment at nine the next morning to help paint the nursery.

Like Ping-Pong balls, her thoughts about that bounced back and forth in her mind.

She didn't want Paul-Anthony there helping paint the room.

Yes, she did, because they would do it together, prepare the nursery for their coming baby like any normal couple.

Ridiculous! They weren't remotely close to having a typical relationship. Didn't now, never would.

But during the hours they painted, it would *seem* as though they did, and she intended to savor and enjoy every minute.

That was foolish and dangerous.

And she was driving herself right out of her already questionable mind.

As Alida entered her outer office, she saw Jerry perched on the edge of Lisa's desk, leaning over and speaking in a low voice to the secretary. When Lisa glanced up, saw Alida and froze, Jerry jumped to his feet.

"Don't let me interrupt," Alida said, managing a small smile. "I'm just passing through."

"How's the little mother?" Jerry asked.

"I'm fine," she said, continuing on toward her office.

"Alida?" Lisa said.

She stopped and turned. "Yes?"

"You look lovely. Really, you do. I like your maternity dress, and there's a glow about you too."

"Thank you, Lisa. I appreciate your saying that."

"I need to see you for a bit, boss," Jerry said.

"Sure. Come on in."

"I'll be there in a minute."

Alida put her purse in the bottom drawer

of her desk, then sat down in her leather chair. Whatever Lisa and Jerry had been discussing, she mused, frowning, they obviously didn't want her to overhear any of it. She'd thought Lisa could barely tolerate Jerry, but they'd certainly appeared very chummy a few minutes earlier. What was the big secret between the two?

Oh, for heaven's sake, she admonished herself. Paul-Anthony's theory that someone could be purposely causing problems with the writers' conference was making her paranoid. Besides, Paul-Anthony had zeroed in on Max, and there she sat casting suspicion on Lisa and Jerry. Pure nonsense.

But then again, she pondered, why would two people who had never gotten along suddenly seem to be the best of buddies? Well, individuals could change. Hadn't Lisa paid her a nice compliment, was, perhaps, making overtures to reestablish their friendship? She certainly hoped so. But did Lisa also intend to change her relationship with Jerry? *What* had they been talking about?

"I'm here," Jerry said, coming into the office. "I took a call that came in for you a few minutes before you got here."

"Oh?"

He settled into a chair. "It was from an editor in New York who's attending the writers' conference. Her publishing company is planning a surprise for the awards banquet on the final night. It's all very hush-hush, with only the awards banquet chairman knowing so she can work it into the program."

"What kind of surprise?"

"A very slick promotion, actually. The editor will announce that each person attending the banquet will receive bound galleys of a blockbuster book they're publishing in December. They'll have people at the doors to hand them out after the banquet."

"Very clever," Alida said, nodding. "The galleys will go home with those who attended and be read all over the country. The people will talk up the book, increase enthusiasm, and that should help the sales of the book when it actually hits the stores."

"Yep. So, here's the scoop. The editor is sending the galleys here to the Swan to your attention. No one, and she emphasized *no one*, is to know about this. Once she and her staff arrive, they'll move the books to their suite, but in the meantime, you're to guard them with your life. That's a direct quote."

Alida smiled. "They're certainly serious about this, aren't they?"

"Very. Lisa knows about it, of course, because she may be the one to sign for the delivery if you're not here. Max should be told, I suppose."

"Well, I suppose," Alida said slowly. Tell

Max? But what if Paul-Anthony was right and Max was behind the problems with the conference? If anything happened to those bound galleys— She stopped herself; she was getting paranoid again. "Of course Max should know. After all, he does come into my office, and he'll wonder why there are boxes stacked against the wall."

"Well, that will be four of us who are in on the deal. No one else should be told." Jerry got to his feet. "I'm off. I have to meet with a guy who's thinking about holding a day-long assertiveness training seminar here. I hope he doesn't practice on me. I hate pushy types. See you later."

"Good-bye for now," Alida said. "Thanks for handling the call from the editor."

"No problem. I'm just glad those galleys are being delivered into *your* care, considering all the screw-ups we've had with this conference. I wouldn't want to be the one baby-sitting those boxes. See ya."

Alida sank back into her chair after he left. Darn it, she thought, now *Jerry* was sounding paranoid. She'd be immensely relieved when those two thousand people had come, gone, and the whole affair was a fait accompli.

With a sigh Alida reached for a file, flipped it open, and got to work.

• • •

Just before nine o'clock the next morning, Paul-Anthony stood outside of Alida's apartment, a deep frown on his face.

He now thoroughly despised his brilliant plan. Acting out the role of a concerned big brother, a man thinking primarily of his baby and hardly at all about the woman carrying it, was driving him right up the wall.

The kiss he and Alida had shared that last night in her apartment proved he was lousy acting the big-brother part. At the slightest provocation he'd hauled Alida into his arms . . . *where she belonged.*

Not only that, he mentally rambled on, while he was admittedly no expert on the whys and wherefores of love, it just didn't seem right that he was introducing subterfuge into such a special and sacred relationship.

Dammit, he thought, what was he going to do? He put together some of the most intricate, complicated investment deals with easy expertise. But when it came to love, he was a complete dud. Alida loved him, he was certain of that, and Lord knew he loved her. It should be a straight line from point A to point B, with a conclusion of "They lived happily ever after." Instead, he was in the middle of a tangled mess, and he didn't know what to do!

"Wing it, Payton," he said. "Play the cards as they're dealt to you."

He knocked on Alida's door. A few moments later she opened it, dressed in maternity jeans and an oversize shirt.

"Hello," she said, smiling up at him. "Are you ready to paint?"

Among other things, he thought dryly. "You bet. I wore my grungiest clothes, and I'm all set to get to it."

She stepped back to allow him to enter. "If you hear a weird noise, it's Scooter. I had to close him up in my bedroom so he couldn't get into the paint. He's not a happy cat. Follow me, sir."

"Anywhere," he said, grinning at her. "Oh, I almost forget," he added. "I love you, Alida."

She stopped and looked at him over her shoulder. "I hope this paint isn't too dark. I want a pale, delicate yellow." She continued on into the spare bedroom.

No doubt about it, Paul-Anthony thought. He really hated his plan.

Alida had everything all set to go. Plastic dropcloths covered the carpeted floor, and in the center of the room was an open can of paint, a paint tray, brushes, and rollers.

Without speaking further, she coated a roller with paint and began applying it to a wall in steady, even strokes. Paul-Anthony did the same, and for the next half hour there was no sound in the room except the squishy noise of paint-coated rollers meeting thirsty walls.

When Paul-Anthony realized he'd been clenching his jaw tighter and tighter with every passing minute, until his teeth ached, he decided enough was enough.

He set the roller in the tray and planted his hands on his hips.

"That's it," he said. "I've had it."

Alida turned to look at him, confusion evident on her face. "Well, okay," she said, shrugging. "If you don't want to paint, that's fine. No one is holding a gun to your head."

He strode across the room to her and gripped her upper arms. "I'm not talking about painting," he said. "Painting is great, a real thrill a minute. But, dammit, Alida, this isn't the room that we should be preparing for our baby."

"It's the only extra room I have. It's a perfectly fine, nice-size room." She paused. "What's wrong with this room?"

"It's here," he said none too quietly.

"What?"

"Alida," he went on, his voice gentling, "I've tried everything I can think of to convince you that I truly love you, will always love you. My latest ridiculous plan was to make you believe that I'd shifted my entire focus from you to the baby, to catch you off guard. I can't play these games anymore."

She stared wordlessly at him.

"I have a huge home," he said, "with room for six babies. Or we can buy a different house that we pick out together. Don't you see? I love you. I want to marry you so we can get on with our lives, be a family. Alida, please, *please*, believe me. I can't fight the ghosts from your past. I just don't know how. All I can do is tell you what's in my heart, my very soul. I want you with me as my wife for the rest of my life."

Two tears slid down Alida's cheeks, quickly followed by two more. She sniffled. "Oh . . . I . . . oh."

"You're very articulate," he said, smiling warmly at her.

"I'm so frightened, Paul-Anthony," she said, trying to halt the flow of tears.

"I understand that, I really do. You've had some rough breaks in the love department in the past, but this is now, and this is me." He released her and raked one hand through his hair. "Look, I'd like to get on a plane, fly to Las Vegas, and be married by tonight, but we'll compromise. All right?"

"Compromise?" she repeated, blinking away her tears.

"Yes. We'll back up a bit. The way we met, what took place on the beach that night in the fog . . . well, it was rather unusual, not your run-of-the-mill getting-to-know-you type of relationship."

"Do tell," she said dryly.

"So, we'll—we'll go out on dates to dinner, concerts, movies, whatever."

"Paul-Anthony, I'm a very pregnant person."

"So? We're doing things a bit out of order, that's all. We need this time together. Well, you need it and I'm agreeing to it. Say yes, Alida. I can't play games for another minute. It's just too damn important. You need time to learn to believe in my love, and you'll have it, but you've got to have an open mind, concentrate on us with no old ghosts allowed to intrude. Will you do it?"

Would she? Alida wondered frantically. Paul-Anthony *hadn't* stopped loving her, *hadn't* shifted his emotions to only the baby. He still loved her and wanted to marry her. Did she dare agree to his compromise, run the risk of heartache once again? Did she dare to hope that maybe, just maybe . . . oh, dear heaven, it was so very frightening.

"Alida, please," he said quietly, "give us a chance. Don't throw us, all we could have together, away before we've even had that chance. Say yes."

Alida felt the baby move within her, as though reminding her that she was not contemplating an answer for herself alone. She was not only eating for two, she was *thinking* for two.

And also to be considered was the fact that she was deeply in love with Paul-Anthony Payton.

"Alida?"

"Yes," she whispered.

He stared up at the ceiling for a long moment. "Thank God." He looked at her again, framing her face in his hands, and brushed his lips over hers. "Now, Miss Hunter, we have a room to finish painting."

She smiled as fresh tears shimmered in her eyes. "We certainly do, Mr. Payton. The paint awaits."

They resumed their task, and within minutes Alida realized she was still smiling. A different aura floated through the room, a quiet sense of contentment as she and Paul-Anthony worked side by side. It was a feeling of togetherness, of sharing, and she basked in the warmth that spread throughout her.

The future was still a hazy blur, but she refused to allow that to dampen her buoyant mood. Paul-Anthony was going to court her, per se, and they'd have a delightful time together. Was it crazy, dangerous, foolish? She didn't care. She felt so alive, and feminine, and loved, and she was going to enjoy every delicious moment of it.

"Oh, my," she said an hour later. "I need a break."

"Good idea," Paul-Anthony said. "That's probably enough physical labor for you for one day. All that's left is the window frame, and I'll do it. You go put your feet up."

"Well . . ."

"Go ahead."

"I should argue the point," she said, laughing, "but I won't. As soon as I get my second wind, I'll make us some lunch."

"No rush. Just rest. Scram."

"Yes, sir."

Their eyes met, and their smiles faded. The atmosphere in the room slowly changed, as though silken, sensual threads were weaving around them. They were preparing a place for a baby, yet their roles of mother and father were nudged into the shadows, leaving only the woman and the man.

As their heartbeats quickened, desire pulsed with increasing intensity within them. Memories assaulted them, vivid memories of the foggy night on the beach, of their exquisite lovemaking.

She loved him so much, Alida thought dreamily. What would he say, what would happen if she declared that love aloud? It was a risk, and did she have the courage . . .

"You are so beautiful," he said softly.

His voice and words jolted her back to reality. She glanced down at her baggy shirt and jeans, which were splattered with paint.

"That's debatable," she said, smiling. "I guess I'd better change clothes before I sit on any furniture. Are you sure you don't mind finishing in here?"

"No problem."

"All right, I'll go. Thank you for helping with the baby's room. It was . . . well, it was . . ." Her voice trailed off.

"I know, I felt it too. You and I, together, were preparing a nursery for our baby. Special, Alida, that's what it was. Very, very special."

She nodded, then turned and hurried out of the room.

Paul-Anthony watched her go, his heart seeming to ache with the force of his love for her. He glanced around the room, seeing it filled with baby furniture, then, smiling, returned to his painting.

Alida took a quick shower, dressed in green slacks and a pleated green and white maternity top. The warm water of the shower had diminished her fatigue, and she went into the kitchen to prepare lunch.

When thick ham sandwiches, drinks, and a bowl of fruit had been set on the table, she called Paul-Anthony. He washed up and joined her in the dining alcove. An indignant Scooter glared at them from the kitchen doorway.

"Don't pout about having been locked in the bedroom," Alida said to the cat. "Yellow isn't your color, and you would have looked grim with it all over you, totally socially unacceptable. Go eat that delicious ham I put in your bowl."

Scooter didn't move.

"He's not a very happy camper," Paul-Anthony said, chuckling.

"I've spoiled him rotten. I'll have to be careful not to spoil the baby like that."

"We won't spoil him, or her. There're lots of books on how to handle various situations. What we don't feel secure about with natural instincts, we'll research."

We, we, we, Alida thought. That sounded so nice, so . . . right. The word came easily to Paul-Anthony, and she'd simply have to get used to hearing it for now, remembering that it was temporary.

"Would you like to go to the zoo tomorrow?" he asked.

"The zoo?"

"Yes, I'm crazy about zoos, but I haven't been to one in more years than I care to think about. It'll be fun."

"The zoo," she repeated. "Well, yes, that does sound like a fun outing. I refuse to go into the snake house, but I could watch the monkeys play for hours, and I adore turtles."

He leaned toward her. "Turtles?"

"Yep," she said, popping a grape into her mouth. "I think they're absolutely fascinating. Turtles are terribly misunderstood creatures. Most people view them as dull, boring, hardly give them a second look. But I think they're extremely intelligent and cute. Very cute. Let's schedule plenty of time for the turtles."

Paul-Anthony laughed. "Sold. I can hardly wait. A whole new experience is about to be presented to me in the form of . . ."

"Turtles," she said firmly, and they laughed together.

Having lost his audience for his award-winning sulk, Scooter went off to eat his ham.

To Alida, the next few weeks seemed to fly by. She was extremely busy at the Swan, and her leisure time was filled to the brim with Paul-Anthony.

They'd had a wonderful time at the zoo, she mused dreamily one afternoon as she sat at her desk. She wasn't certain Paul-Anthony was now a true-blue admirer of turtles, but he'd given appreciation of the funny creatures his best shot.

On another night they'd gone to a concert. Two evenings had been spent at her apartment, cooking dinner together, then watching old movies on television. They'd gone shopping, to museums, on long drives out of the city.

And Paul-Anthony, she thought, her cheeks flushing with warmth, was always the one who ended the searing kiss they shared before he left her apartment. In the month since they'd painted the nursery, he was the one who made certain their ever-increasing desire did not rage out of control.

Alida leaned back in her chair and smiled up at the ceiling. Such glorious days and dream-filled nights she was having. Paul-Anthony was attentive and charming. He listened to every word she said, asked her opinions, and inquired, but didn't nag, about the care she was taking of herself and the baby. They never ran out of things to talk about, yet when a silence did fall between them, it was comfortable.

Alida sighed. She loved Paul-Anthony so very much. More and more often now, she found herself fantasizing about what it would be like to be his wife. They'd raise this child and others they'd create. They'd be a family, always together.

"Sleeping on the job?" a voice said.

Alida sat up. "Oh, hi, Lisa. No, I wasn't sleeping, I was . . ." She laughed. "I was having a mental conversation with myself, which is probably as certifiably insane as talking aloud to myself. The truth be known, I'm a cuckoo."

"I talk to myself all the time. If you're nutty, then so am I. Listen, I have a delivery man out here with the boxes of the galleys from the publisher. Where do you want them?"

"Have him bring them in here and stack

them against that wall over there. I'll have to
stare at them for a week until the editor gets
here for the conference. I'll be so glad when
this affair is over."

"Amen to that," Lisa said.

That evening Alida dressed in jeans and a
casual maternity top, per Paul-Anthony's instructions. They were going out to dinner,
he'd told her, but comfortable clothes were
the order of the day.

He arrived promptly at seven o'clock, and
took her into his arms as soon as he entered
the apartment.

"Hello," she said, smiling.

"Hello to you." He kissed her deeply, then
raised his head. "Could you speak to the ju-
nior member of this firm about the way he
kicks me every time I kiss you? Let's have a
little respect here."

She laughed. "I'll send him a memo."

"Ready to go?"

"Yes, but where are we going?"

"You'll see. You'd better bring a sweater.
It's a bit nippy out."

The October night was, indeed, chilly, and
Alida snuggled into the plush leather seat of
Paul-Anthony's car. They chatted as he drove,
Alida telling him that the galleys had arrived
from New York.

"I assume they're locked up tight," he said, glancing at her.

She nodded. "They're in my office."

"Well, I guess the things that went wrong earlier were just a fluke. Nothing else has happened for weeks now."

"I know, but I'm still nervous about it. I'll be glad when that conference is over."

Paul-Anthony nodded.

Alida fell silent, paying more attention to where they were going. They were now in an exclusive neighborhood that boasted large houses set back from the street, fronted by sloping, perfectly manicured lawns. Minutes later Paul-Anthony turned into a driveway, drove up the incline, and shut off the ignition.

"I thought it was time you saw my home," he said quietly.

"Oh, my Lord," she murmured. "It's huge."

"Let's go in."

Lights glowed on the first floor of the two-story house. Alida passed through the wide entryway into the living room, her gaze sweeping over the enormous area.

A flagstone fireplace topped by a dark wood mantel covered nearly one entire wall. The carpeting was deep gold, the furniture upholstered in brown, oatmeal, gold, and green. The overall effect was one of obvious opulence, yet had a welcoming warmth to it.

"Magnificent," she said, not realizing she'd spoken aloud.

"I'll give you a tour of the rest of it," Paul-Anthony said from behind her, "then our dinner should be ready. Because I love you, I'm not subjecting you to my cooking. My housekeeper prepared a casserole and what have you before she went home."

Alida ran out of things to say as he led her from one room to the next. Mere words, she decided, weren't adequate to describe her reaction to Paul-Anthony's home. It was so beautiful, and had been decorated with such care and attention to detail.

There were six bedrooms upstairs—six! —and the downstairs boasted a formal dining room, a library, a family room with an extensive home-entertainment center, and two bathrooms. The kitchen had every modern appliance imaginable, and at one end of the large room, an eating area was set into the alcove of a bay window.

Paul-Anthony waved her onto a chair by the window and brought the bubbling casserole to the table. The refrigerator produced a crisp tossed salad. An apple pie beckoned from beneath a glass dome on the counter.

"Help yourself," he said as he sat down opposite her.

She did, and they ate in silence for several minutes.

"Alida," Paul-Anthony said finally, "do you like the house?"

She looked up at him. "Oh, yes, of course I do. It's lovely. Yes, I like it very much."

"I purposely postponed bringing you here with the hope that when you did come, you'd view it not through the eyes of someone just visiting for a few hours but . . . Look, maybe you're not ready to hear this yet, but as wonderful as these past weeks have been, we simply can't go on like this indefinitely."

"Paul-Anthony . . ."

"No, let me finish, okay? Alida, I want very much for us to be married before the baby is born, so he'll come into this world with my name as well as my love."

"But I—"

He raised one hand to silence her. "We can live here, or buy a different place if you'd rather. I know I helped paint the nursery at your apartment and I have special memories of that day. But, Alida, you and our baby don't belong there. We're a family, the three of us. You can get out from beneath Max Brewer's thumb and—"

"Wait a minute. What are you saying?"

"You don't have to work for that cretin, be forced to function under that kind of stress. You'll be busy with the baby once it arrives."

"Paul-Anthony, it's possible to combine a career with motherhood. Millions of women do it. I've worked very hard to achieve my goals, and I have no intention of quitting my job. I'll have a maternity leave, then return to the Swan. The time I spend with the baby will be of the highest quality. That's much better than quantity, when you consider that I need my job to make me the complete woman I am now. The baby won't suffer neglect from having a working mother."

"I think a mother belongs with her children, at least until they start school."

"Not in every instance, Paul-Anthony, don't you see that? If I'm unhappy, not fulfilled, I won't be a good mother." She shook her head. "This conversation is crazy. We started out talking about houses, and now we're having a debate on working mothers."

"Not working mothers in general. You. The mother of my child, *my* wife—"

"Paul-Anthony," she said, pushing herself to her feet, "I am *not* your wife."

He lunged out of his chair. "You would be by now if you weren't so damn stubborn. We could get married immediately, you could move in here, and we'd be totally prepared for our baby when it arrives."

"Providing I quit my job, of course," she said, her voice rising as loud as his. "I have no intention of doing that. So, now what, Paul-Anthony? Did I flunk the wife interview, not measure up to your preconceived standards? Is that going to be the reasoning behind your dusting me off? Well, don't waste your breath telling me it's over. I knew it was coming. I just didn't know when. Now I do."

"Dammit, Alida, stop it. We've hit a glitch, that's all. We can work this out."

"How? It's all very black and white with no gray area for compromise. You want me to give up my career. I refuse to do that. The end." Hot tears burned her eyes. "The end. I'll—I'll phone for a taxi. I'm going home."

"*This* is your home!" he roared.

"No," she said quietly. "No, it isn't."

He raked one hand through his hair. "Ah, hell, what a mess. There's no use trying to discuss this anymore tonight. I'll take you to your apartment. Do notice I didn't say 'home.' But we're not finished, Alida. Not by a long shot." He strode from the room.

"Yes, we are," she whispered. "It was temporary, the love, the caring. And now it's over."

Eight

The remainder of the week, through the weekend, and on into the beginning of the next
week, Alida mentally labeled herself a study
in misery. She loved Paul-Anthony, missed
Paul-Anthony, and, despite her firm resolve to
be prepared for the end of their relationship,
was suffering the anguish of heartache.

Once again, she admonished herself continually, she had done a lousy job of loving.
She'd been foolish to believe she could love
for a short time, then retreat to her safe emotional haven unscathed.

And niggling at her mind were doubts as
well. The scene in Paul-Anthony's kitchen replayed itself every day, causing her to question the validity of what she'd said and done.

Had she been too hasty in deciding what she had with Paul-Anthony was over, she asked herself. At the emergence of the first "glitch," as he had called it, she'd immediately assumed their relationship had reached its inevitable end. She hadn't even considered trying to reach a compromise regarding her career. Paul-Anthony had still been declaring his love for her as she was telling him that they were finished.

Maybe she'd been wrong. Maybe there was still a chance . . .

No, no, she'd quickly tell herself, she was right. If it hadn't been her career, then a disagreement over something else would have demolished what they shared.

But then again . . .

On it went, the confusion raging in her mind until she was both physically and emotionally exhausted.

Alida sighed as she attempted to concentrate on the stack of letters she had to answer.

"Alida," Lisa said, coming into the office, "it's time to go home."

"What? Oh, it is, isn't it? Darn, I need to finish the bid for that bankers' convention. I'll take the file home with me, I guess."

"Is it that urgent? You look very tired. Are you all right?"

"Yes, I'm fine." Alida's gaze swept over the boxes of galleys stacked against the wall. "The editor will arrive tomorrow to take possession of those nuisances, thank goodness. That will be one thing off my mind. Are you leaving now?"

"I . . . um, no, not quite yet. I'm expecting a phone call. Well, you go on home. Good night."

" 'Night," Alida said absently.

Halfway across the parking lot, Alida stopped with a shake of her head. She'd walked off without the file she was going to work on at home. Her brain definitely wasn't working on all cylinders.

She turned and trudged back into the hotel. As she approached the open door to Lisa's office, she heard the telephone ring, then Lisa's cheerful greeting.

"Oh, hello, Paul-Anthony," she said. "I was waiting for your call, and your timing is perfect. Alida just left the hotel."

Alida halted abruptly.

"No," Lisa went on, "she doesn't suspect a thing, I'm certain of it. I've been very careful about what I've said to her."

Oh, dear heaven, Alida thought, closing her eyes as a wave of dizziness swept over her.

"Yes, I know Alida's been concerned about the galleys," Lisa said, "but there soon won't be any galleys to worry about. You have my spare key to the office, right? . . . Yes, yes, fine. We make a terrific team, Paul-Anthony.

I'll talk to you later. . . . Yes, I feel the same way. 'Bye."

Hearing Lisa hang up, Alida spun around and raced down the hall, tears blurring her vision. When she reached her car, she sped away from the hotel, her knuckles white from her tight hold on the steering wheel.

She refused to think. She just blanked her mind and drove, scarcely aware of the heavy rush hour traffic. She didn't know where she was going. Nor did she care.

Nearly an hour later she flicked on the blinker and exited off the expressway. A few minutes later she pulled into a parking lot and shut off the ignition.

She felt as though she were emerging from a dream. She had driven to the beach where she'd first met Paul-Anthony in the fog.

Her legs trembling, she walked across the beach to the edge of the water. Her gaze swept over the peaceful ocean, then up to the sky, streaked with the vivid colors of the sunset. She started slowly down the beach, one hand resting protectively on her protruding stomach.

Lisa and Paul-Anthony, she forced herself to think. Paul-Anthony and Lisa. It was all so clear now, horrifyingly clear. Paul-Anthony wanted custody of the baby. If she married him, he'd probably file for divorce as soon as the baby was born, then use his power and money to gain possession of their child. And if she didn't have a job, no means of support, his case would be even stronger. It had been Paul-Anthony and Lisa who had engineered the mishaps with the writers' conference.

And, oh, dear Lord, Paul-Anthony was going to steal the galleys!

They were a terrific team, Lisa had said, and Alida hadn't suspected a thing. "I feel the same way," Lisa had cooed. Meaning what? That they loved each other? Yes, it fit. It all came together like a gruesome picture of an intricate puzzle.

Alida stopped walking and pressed shaking fingers to her lips as tears slipped from her eyes.

Betrayed. She'd been betrayed by the man she'd dared to love. Oh, God, she was such a fool. She'd stood on that very beach the night of April Fool's Day and declared herself to be the greatest fool of all.

And she was.

She had loved again, and lost again. Excruciating pain seared her very soul.

Time passed unnoticed and darkness fell as Alida stood alone, wrapped in a shroud of misery. A chill wind swept across the water, and she shivered, the cold air jarring her from her tormented thoughts. She dashed the tears from her cheeks and lifted her chin.

Paul-Anthony Payton, she decided with a flash of anger, was *not* going to take those galleys. And Paul-Anthony Payton was *not* going to take *her* baby.

Quickly, she returned to her car, then drove to the hotel, drumming her fingers impatiently on the steering wheel at each red light, each minor traffic jam.

Her anger overshadowed the painful heartache, dulling it in a temporary reprieve. With the fury of a betrayed woman, she vowed to protect those galleys and, therefore, her career. And with the fury of a mother, she vowed to protect her child.

At the Swan, Alida quickly checked the parking lot and saw that Lisa's car was no longer there. Inside the building, she found Lisa's office door securely locked. She let herself in and locked the door behind her.

Without turning on the lights she crossed to her own office door. Again she locked the door behind her, then stood still until her eyes adjusted to the darkness. The boxes of galleys were against the wall, undisturbed.

She sank into her chair with an exhausted sigh . . . and waited.

During the next two hours, memories of the glorious time she'd spent with Paul-Anthony haunted her. In her mind's eye she saw his handsome face, his smile, his sky-blue eyes. She could hear his laughter, the rich timbre of his voice as he said, again and again, "I love you, Alida."

Those memories, she knew, were to have been precious treasures to savor when Paul-Anthony left her. But now they were tormenting reminders of her foolishness.

Alida placed her hands on her stomach and tried desperately to concentrate on the baby, *her* baby. But that night, as she sat in the darkness waiting for Paul-Anthony's final betrayal, not even her child brought her comfort.

Suddenly she stiffened as she heard a noise in the outer office. She got to her feet and moved silently to the side of the door, one hand pressed over her wildly beating heart.

A key was inserted in the lock on her office door, and she had to remind herself to breathe as she saw the knob turn. The door opened slowly, then the room was set ablaze with light. She blinked several times against the glaring intrusion.

The door was shut, revealing the man who'd opened it. A sob caught in Alida's throat.

"Oh, Paul-Anthony," she said, her voice filled with her fatigue and sadness.

He spun around, obviously shocked to see her. He shut the door and started toward her. She stepped back.

"Alida, for heaven's sake," he said, "what on earth are you doing here, hiding in the dark like this?" He paused. "The galleys. You're trying to protect the galleys, aren't you?"

"Yes!" she cried. "I'm protecting the galleys from you, Paul-Anthony Payton."

"What?"

"Oh, please, don't insult me further by pretending you have no idea what I'm talking about. I heard Lisa speaking to you on the telephone earlier. She was right. I didn't suspect a thing, not then. But now I see the whole sordid, ugly picture. You and Lisa lose, Paul-Anthony, because you're not touching those galleys."

"You think I came here to . . . dammit, Alida—"

"No, damn *you*, Paul-Anthony. You'll stop at nothing to assure that things go the way you want them to. You tried plan after plan to convince me that you love me, would always love me, and none of them worked. So, desperate measures were called for, and you found the perfect partner in Lisa. She's angry and hurt because she feels I didn't treat our friendship as I should. She's very attracted to you, and you used that too."

She drew in a quick breath, hoping to steady her voice. "You're a despicable man, Paul-Anthony, and so very clever. Max would fire me the moment it was discovered those galleys were gone. There I'd be, out of a job with no means to support my child. I'd agree to marry you, you'd divorce me, and gain custody of the baby. Or, if that was too messy, you could simply go to court for custody without brothering to marry me at all."

"'That's what you honestly believe?" he asked quietly.

"Yes, because it all fits, it all adds up. I'm a fool, just as I said on the beach that night. I dared to love again . . ." She swiped at the few tears that seeped from her eyes. "I fell so deeply in love with you, and you were a walking, talking, living lie. Get out of this office, and out of my life! Go away, Paul-Anthony, and leave me in peace."

"Alida, for God's sake, I—" He stopped abruptly, then swung around and hit the light switch, turning off the lights. "Shh," he whispered, creeping back to her. "I heard something. Yes, listen. Someone just came into Lisa's office." He circled Alida's shoulders with his arm and held her close to his side.

Alida started to struggle out of his grasp, then froze in fear as her office door swung open. Again the room came alive with light.

"Well, well, well," Paul-Anthony said, "look who's here."

"Jerry," Alida whispered.

Jerry quickly glanced over his shoulder toward Lisa's office, then turned back to Alida and Paul-Anthony.

"Genius minds working on the same wavelength," he said, flashing a smile. "I assume you're baby-sitting the galleys. Well, that's exactly why *I'm* here. Can't let anything happen to those books, you know." He glanced over his shoulder again. "You two can take off. I'll stay here and play bodyguard."

"No, I don't think so," Paul-Anthony said. "As a matter of fact, Jerry, I'm having a problem with your showing up like this."

"Why?" Jerry asked, his smile fading into a frown. "I just told you the reason I came."

Paul-Anthony nodded. "The galleys."

"That's right. Alida, you look beat. You should be home with your feet up."

"So you'll be free to steal the books?" Paul-Anthony asked. "Or maybe cancel your plans so you don't get caught?"

Alida shook her head, distress clouding her eyes. "Paul-Anthony, are you saying that Jerry . . ."

"It fits," Paul-Anthony said. "If you got fired, Jerry is next up for the director position. Right, Nash?"

"You're crazy, Payton," Jerry said, "and you don't have one bit of proof." He glanced into Lisa's office again and stiffened. "Well, if you're determined to stay," he went on, smiling thinly, "there's no sense in my being here too. I'm leaving. I'll forget what you accused me of, Payton. No hard feelings."

"Hold it," Paul-Anthony said. He strode across the room and looked past Jerry into Lisa's office. "Come join the party."

Alida gasped as a short, thin man pushed a metal dolly into her office. "Who are you?" she asked.

The man ignored her, turning to Jerry. "Hey, am I doin' this job, or not?" He glanced at Paul-Anthony. "This here guy hired me and my truck to pick up some boxes. Don't bother me none what time of day it is, long as I get paid in advance. I got my cash, so where's the stuff?"

"Keep the money," Paul-Anthony said, "but there's nothing here for you to take."

The man shrugged. "Fine by me." He left the office, dragging the dolly behind him.

"Damn you, Payton," Jerry said fiercely. "I had this planned down to the last detail. Everything has gone perfectly until now."

Alida stared at Jerry. "*You* were behind all those problems with the writers' conference? You sent the wrong instructions to the printer, rerouted the tote bags? And you're here to steal the galleys? Dear heaven, Jerry, why?"

"Because I should have had your job in the first place!" he yelled. "I almost quit then, when it was given to you, but I decided to bide my time, wait for the situation I needed to get you fired. You cooperated nicely by getting pregnant. Max is helping me without realizing it because he wants you out of here too. The galleys were my crowning glory. You'd be booted out tomorrow, and I'd have the position that is rightfully mine."

"Oh, Jerry, I can't believe this," Alida said, shaking her head. "I had no idea you resented me so much, that you've been acting out a role all this time."

"The curtain just came down on the performance," Paul-Anthony said. "Have your resignation on Max Brewer's desk first thing in the morning, Nash. You're finished here. Don't give one second's thought to trying to lie your way out of this because you'll answer to me. Clear?"

Jerry's face flushed red with fury, and he took a step toward Paul-Anthony. Then with an earthy expletive he turned and stalked out of the office, slamming the door behind him.

A heavy silence fell over the room.

Alida slowly faced Paul-Anthony, who stood with his arms crossed over his chest, an unreadable expression on his face.

"I—I owe you an apology," she said quietly.

He nodded. "Yes, you do."

"Well, I'm sorry, but when I heard what Lisa said to you on the phone, I—" She threw up her hands.

"Ah, yes, the incriminating phone call. Let's see. She said you didn't suspect a thing, and you still don't . . . about the baby shower she's planning for you. I'm in on it so that I'll have you in the right place at the right time. It's Lisa's way of letting you know how much she values your friendship."

"Oh," Alida said in a small voice.

"What else? Oh, my having her keys. Well, I

needed them to get in here to guard the galleys. Why? Because I was wrong. Old-fashioned, chauvinistic, and wrong. Careers and motherhood *can* be combined, and I was going to make certain that nothing happened to your job."

"Oh."

"I seem to remember Lisa agreeing that she felt the same way I did. Are you curious as to what that was all about? Sure, you are. I said you were a very special, wonderful woman, and I loved you very much. Lisa said she felt the same way."

"Oh."

"So! That clears that up, and now I have a question for you." He started slowly toward her. "While you were accusing me of my various crimes, you said that you had fallen deeply in love with me. Is that true, Alida?" He stopped in front of her and gently cupped her face in his hands. "Is it?"

"Yes, but . . ."

"And now do you believe that I love you, will always love you? Do you know I love you and our baby, and want us to be a family? Alida Hunter, have I, at long last, convinced you that you are my life and should be my wife for all time?"

"Oh, yes, yes, you have," she said, grasping his shoulders. "But now I've ruined everything. Dear heaven, Paul-Anthony, how can you love someone who thought the worst of you, didn't trust or believe in you? Won't you always wonder when I'll next doubt you, question what you've done or said?"

"No, my darling, I won't, because all of this is being put to rest, along with your ghosts of the past. Besides, given the evidence you had, I looked guilty as sin for a while there. We're staring fresh, right now, from this minute forward. Alida, will you marry me? Please?"

"Yes, I'll marry you," she said, smiling through her tears. "I love you, Paul-Anthony Payton. I will love you forever. From the moment we met, you've been *my* man of the mist."

She thought she glimpsed tears shimmering in his eyes, then he lowered his head and kissed her with such intensity, a mist seemed to float around them, encasing them in a private world of love.

Epilogue

Paul-Anthony pushed open the hospital room door and stood quietly for a moment. Alida was sitting up in bed, holding a blanket-wrapped bundle in the crook of her arm, a soft smile on her lips.

"Beautiful," he said.

She looked up, and her smile widened. "Hello, darling. We've been waiting for you. I just had a long conversation with our son, and he's not feeling a bit guilty about our postponing opening our gifts because he decided to be born on Christmas Day."

Paul-Anthony crossed the room and kissed Alida, then gazed at the sleeping baby, who had a rosy complexion and a cap of dark, silky hair.

"He's so small," he said.

"Paul-Anthony, eight pounds two ounces is *not* small. I can hardly wait to go home tomorrow."

"You just want to get at your Christmas presents," he said, chuckling.

"Of course I do. The tree looks so beautiful in your living room."

"*Our* living room."

She smiled. "*Our* living room, in *our* home."

The baby opened his eyes.

"Hey, hello, kiddo," Paul-Anthony said. "Remember me? I'm your dad. And you, young sir, are Chris-Noel Payton. That's with a hyphen, sport, in Payton tradition."

The door burst open and John-Trevor strode in with a huge stuffed dog under one arm.

"Hi, Chris-Noel," he said. "Oh, hello, Alida, Paul-Anthony. I wanted to see my nephew once more before I left for the airport."

"Business or pleasure trip, John-Trevor?" Alida asked.

"Business, all business. There's an eccentric old guy I do work for periodically, who will deal only with me personally." He shrugged. "I like the feisty buzzard, so I humor him. Anyhow, I'm winging my way to Colorado to see what little chore he's got for me this time. Hey, Chris-Noel, wake up and look at this terrific dog. Oh, well." He pushed the toy into Paul-Anthony's arms, then kissed Alida on the forehead. "What are you planning to do for next Christmas? Chris-Noel will be a tough act to follow."

"Well," Alida said slowly, "it should be your turn to liven up the holidays, John-Trevor. We could all attend your Christmas wedding."

"I'm out of here," he said, striding toward the door. "That kind of talk makes me break out in hives. Happy New Year, y'all." The door swished closed behind him.

"Happy New Year," Alida said to Paul-Anthony.

"We'll have a lifetime of happy years, my love. In sunshine-filled days, and nights of our private . . ."

". . . mist," she finished for him, then stopped speaking to receive his kiss.

Chris-Noel Payton slept on.

THE EDITOR'S CORNER

As you look forward to the holiday season—the most romantic season of all—you can plan on enjoying some of the very best love stories of the year from LOVESWEPT. Our authors know that not all gifts come in boxes wrapped in pretty paper and tied with bows. In fact, the most special gifts are the gifts that come from the heart, and in each of the six LOVESWEPTs next month, characters are presented with unique gifts that transform their lives through love.

Whenever we publish an Iris Johansen love story, it's an event! In **AN UNEXPECTED SONG,** LOVE-SWEPT #438, Iris's hero, Jason Hayes, is mesmerized by the lovely voice of singer Daisy Justine and realizes instantly that she was born to sing his music. But Daisy has obligations that mean more to her than fame and fortune. She desperately wants the role he offers, but even more she wants to be touched, devoured by the tormented man who tangled his fingers in her hair. Jason bestows upon Daisy the gift of music from his soul, and in turn she vows to capture his heart and free him from the darkness where he's lived for so long. This hauntingly beautiful story is a true treat for all lovers of romance from one of the genre's premier authors.

In **SATURDAY MORNINGS,** LOVESWEPT #439, Peggy Webb deals with a different kind of gift, the gift of belonging. To all observers, heroine Margaret Leigh Jones is a proper, straitlaced librarian who seems content with her life—until she meets outrageous rogue Andrew McGill when she brings him her poodle to train. Then she wishes she knew how to flirt instead of how to blush! And Andrew's
(continued)

peaceful Saturday mornings are never the same after Margaret Leigh learns a shocking family secret that sends her out looking for trouble and for ways to hone her womanly wiles. All of Andrew's possessive, protective instincts rush to the fore as he falls head over heels for this crazy, vulnerable woman who tries just a bit too hard to be brazen. Through Andrew's love Margaret Leigh finally sees the error of her ways and finds the answer to the questions of who she really is and where she belongs—as Andrew's soul mate, sharing his Saturday mornings forever.

Wonderful storyteller Lori Copeland returns next month with another lighthearted romp, **'TIZ THE SEASON,** LOVESWEPT #440. Hero Cody Benderman has a tough job ahead of him in convincing Darby Piper that it's time for her to fall in love. The serious spitfire of an attorney won't budge an inch at first, when the undeniably tall, dark, and handsome construction foreman attempts to turn her orderly life into chaos by wrestling with her in the snow, tickling her breathless beside a crackling fire—and erecting a giant holiday display that has Darby's clients up in arms. But Darby gradually succumbs to Cody's charm, and she realizes he's given her a true gift of love—the gift of discovering the simple joys in life and taking the time to appreciate them. She knows she'll never stop loving or appreciating Cody!

LOVESWEPT #441 by Terry Lawrence is a sensuously charged story of **UNFINISHED PASSION.** Marcie Courville and Ray Crane meet again as jurors on the same case, but much has changed in the ten years since the ruggedly sexy construction worker had awakened the desire of the pretty, privi-

(continued)

leged young woman. In the intimate quarters of the jury room, each feels the sparks that still crackle between them, and each reacts differently. Ray knows he can still make Marcie burn with desire—and now he has so much more to offer her. Marcie knows she made the biggest mistake of her life when she broke Ray's heart all those years ago. But how can she erase the past? Through his love for her, Ray is able to give Marcie a precious gift—the gift of rectifying the past—and Marcie is able to restore the pride of the first man she ever loved, the only man she ever loved. Rest assured there's no unfinished passion between these two when the happy ending comes!

Gail Douglas makes a universal dream come true in **IT HAD TO BE YOU**, LOVESWEPT #442. Haven't you ever dreamed of falling in love aboard a luxury cruise ship? I can't think of a more romantic setting than the *QE2*. For Mike Harris it's love at first sight when he spots beautiful nymph Caitlin Grant on the dock. With her endless legs and sea-green eyes, Caitlin is his male fantasy come true—and he intends to make the most of their week together at sea. For Caitlin the gorgeous stranger in the Armani suit seems to be a perfect candidate for a shipboard romance. But how can she ever hope for more with a successful doctor who will never be able to understand her wanderer's spirit and the joy she derives from taking life as it comes? Caitlin believes she is following her heart's desire by traveling and experiencing life to the fullest—until her love for Mike makes her realize her true desire. He gives her restless heart the gift of a permanent home in his arms—and she promises to stay forever.

(continued)

Come along for the ride as psychologist Maya Stephens draws Wick McCall under her spell in **DEEPER AND DEEPER**, LOVESWEPT #443, by Jan Hudson. The sultry-eyed enchantress who conducts the no-smoking seminar has a voice that pours over Wick like warm honey, but the daredevil adventurer can't convince the teacher to date a younger man. Maya spends her days helping others overcome their problems, but she harbors secret terrors of her own. When Wick challenges her to surrender to the wildness beneath the cool facade she presents to the world, she does, reveling in his sizzling caresses and drowning in the depths of his tawny-gold eyes. For the first time in her life Maya is able to truly give of herself to another—not as a teacher to a student, but as a woman to a man, a lover to her partner—and she has Wick to thank for that. He's shown her it's possible to love and not lose, and to give everything she has and not feel empty inside, only fulfilled.

Enjoy next month's selection of LOVESWEPTs, while you contemplate what special gifts from the heart you'll present to those you love this season!

Sincerely,

Susann Brailey

Susann Brailey
Editor
LOVESWEPT
Bantam Books
666 Fifth Avenue
New York, NY 10103

FOREVER LOVESWEPT
SPECIAL KEEPSAKE EDITION OFFER
SELECTION FORM

Choose from these special Loveswepts by your favorite authors. Please write a 1 next to your first choice, a 2 next to your second choice. Loveswept will honor your preference as inventory allows.

Loveswept ®

_____BAD FOR EACH OTHER   Billie Green

_____NOTORIOUS   Iris Johansen

_____WILD CHILD   Suzanne Forster

_____A WHOLE NEW LIGHT   Sandra Brown

_____HOT TOUCH   Deborah Smith

_____ONCE UPON A TIME...GOLDEN

THREADS   Kay Hooper

Attached are 15 hearts and the selection form which indicates my choices for my special hardcover Loveswept "Keepsake Edition." Please mail my book to:

NAME:_____

ADDRESS:_____

CITY/STATE:_____ZIP:_____

Offer open only to residents of the United States, Puerto Rico and Canada. Void where prohibited, taxed, or restricted. Allow 6 - 8 weeks after receipt of coupons for delivery. Offer expires January 15, 1991. You will receive your first choice as inventory allows; if that book is no longer available, you'll receive your second choice, etc.

"Hello, Alida," Paul-Anthony said quietly.

"No," she whispered, staring at him with wide eyes.

"It wasn't easy finding you, but I finally managed it."

"Why?" she asked. "What do you want with me?"

"Don't you know?" he said. "What happened to us on the beach that night was fantastic, wonderful, and very, very important."

"It wasn't real," she said fiercely. "Forget that it happened."

"Alida, you told me that night to pay attention, and the special woman who was meant to be mine wouldn't pass me by unnoticed. Well, I've found that special lady . . . and her name is Alida Hunter. I have no intention of losing you because I waited too long. You're mine, or you will be as soon as you stop fighting me every inch of the way. We joined our hearts and souls that night, don't you remember?"

A thrumming heat pulsed deep within her as she was held immobile under the mesmerizing gaze of Paul-Anthony's blue eyes. Vivid pictures of the time they'd spent together on the foggy beach flashed before her eyes, made her heart race and her cheeks flush. She had only to lift her hands to touch him once again, to feel his powerful body. He was so close . . . so close—

"No! I won't lose my heart to another man. Not ever again," she vowed.

"I see I'll have to remind you what happened between us," Paul-Anthony said. In a sudden move that left her no escape, he pulled her into his arms, and kissed her with total abandon. . . .

WHAT ARE *LOVESWEPT* ROMANCES?

They are stories of true romance and touching emotion. We believe those two very important ingredients are constants in our highly sensual and very believable stories in the *LOVESWEPT* line. Our goal is to give you, the reader, stories of consistently high quality that may sometimes make you laugh, sometimes make you cry, but are always fresh and creative and contain many delightful surprises within their pages.

Most romance fans read an enormous number of books. Those they truly love, they keep. Others may be traded with friends and soon forgotten. We hope that each *LOVESWEPT* romance will be a treasure—a "keeper." We will always try to publish

LOVE STORIES YOU'LL NEVER FORGET
BY AUTHORS YOU'LL ALWAYS REMEMBER

The Editors